The Revenge of a 17th century witch

by Linda Louisa Dell

Disclaimer

Alice Park was a real person who was charged and convicted of witchcraft, and hanged in the late sixteenth century, she died and left a young daughter. The rest or this story is fiction and the characters are not based on real people living of dead.

In 1563 the law was changed, and enchantment and witchcraft were made a capital offence.

Much of my story takes place in an England plagued by the witch hunters, such as the notorious, Matthew Hopkins Witch Finder General. The persecution of witches and people of different faiths became endemic over this period of history.

In the seventeenth century when King James the 1st came to the throne, he wrote his book Demonology which actually sought to prevent wrongful conviction of witches. However, since most of his subjects could not read. They saw the book as a royal sanction for the persecution of witches and hedge wives. This was also a time when petty or malicious grievances could escalate into charges of witchcraft and the subsequent death of many innocent women.

Other books by Linda Louisa Dell

Non fiction

Can't Sleep Won't Sleep (Reasons and remedies for insomnia) Published in 2005

Dreamtime (A History, Mythology, Physiology and Guide to the Interpretation and A-Z of Dreams) Published in 2008

Aphrodisiacs, Aphrodite's Secrets (Sexuality, Sexual Dysfunction and an A-Z, History and Anecdotal use of Aphrodisiacs) Published in 2009

Aphrodisiacs (an a-z) Skyhorse publishing, New York

Jokes (a collection of jokes)

Who said that? (Meanings and origins of popular sayings)

Mystic Moon (A history of the mythology, astrology and spiritual significance of the Moon)

Fiction

Rosie's Story (if pigs could fly)

African Nights (Georgina's Story)

Earthscape, (a long way from home)

The Arranged wedding

Chapter one

May 17th 1558 Exeter Crown Court

They came to my cell to take me to the gallows at ten in the morning.

I was still weak and traumatized because, at the beginning of my incarceration I had not been allowed to sleep for days on end. When I fainted, they would throw cold water over me and make me walk again.

I was walked back and forwards across the room by two men, back and forwards all night and all day with no respite.

I thought that I would lose my reason. I was given no food and very little to drink. Every so often we would stop and one of the men would question me.

"Just tell us and it will end, you are a witch? Who else is in your coven?"

I told them I knew nothing about witches or covens, but they would not let me rest. At one time I think my mind just shut down, then they would make me sit on a three-legged stool and they would search my body for the signs of the Devil. I once came to consciousness abruptly as they stuck this needle into my side.

They poked me again and there was no pain.

"See," said the taller man, "the sign of the devil," but it was just a mole on my skin below my breast.

Then the walking started again, until I collapsed and could not move, they tried to drag me up and across the floor, but soon gave up and let me collapse into a heap. Then it seemed that weeks had passed. I lived on somehow, on a little dry bread and a cup of water a day, until today.

I am led, struggling, to the yard of the prison, where I can see the platform and the hangman waiting. As I stumble up the stairs, he reaches out for me and said, "Be brave Alice, it will soon be over."

As I stand there on trembling legs the noose is put over my head.

"Who will look after my daughter?" I ask.

"She is alright. A couple in the village have taken her in," he said. "Be at peace now."

Then I felt the rope tighten around my neck and the noise of the trapdoor. There was a moment when my feet were kicking in air and I felt the rope choking me and then oblivion.

Chapter two

London, Sloane Square March 1959

Witch Queen Emelia Rey had a lot on her mind as she reclined in the luxury of her palatial town house in London's Sloane Square.

"Would you ask Alana to come and see me," she asked her assistant, as she stroked her pet black panther Ebony. He rubbed himself against Emelia legs but then retreaded over to his comfortable bed by the window when Hermosa came nearer.

"Yes, your majesty," Hermosa replied, keeping a sharp look out of the corner of her eye at the big cat.

"Get Kigali to feed Ebony would you, while I am talking to Alana?"

The Queens attendants were not very fond of the queen's pet cat, who could get a bit temperamental if he was not cosseted and fed on demand. As Ebony was led away, Alana entered the room.

"Ah, Alana. I have had a request from someone called Jilly Longland, she has contacted via the coven in Moeston. They seem to be having some problems in the village of Little Barnstead."

"Where is Little Barnstead?" Alana asked.

"It's a little sixteenth century English village, on the edge of Dartmoor, the village Little Barnstead has a lot of history and at least three witches were killed from there over the years."

"So, what do they think is the problem?" Alana asked.

"Back in the sixteenth century a witch, one Maud Park Longland, put a curse on the local aristocratic family. They think that someone is trying to re-activate that curse."

"How can I appear in the village without being too conspicuous?" Alana asked.

"I have thought of that. One of our members, Wanda, runs a gift shop in the village but she wants to retire. I am thinking that you can go in there as the new proprietor, of the shop."

"What is the shop called?" Alana asked.

"The shop is called Pandoras Box, and it carries a range of esoteric goods, as far as I am aware it does a small but lucrative business."

"That could be fun, when would you want me to go?"

"As soon as possible. I could get Kigali to drive you down at the weekend. Wanda is keen to move out as soon as possible, she is going to live with her sister in Cornwall. But she will wait for you to arrive to show you around, explain a few things and hand over the keys." Emelia Rey said. "Do you want to take this assignment? It would get you away from the problems you have caused here with your folly and bad judgment."

"I will go, and I will try to get to the bottom of the situation, your majesty," Alana said. "Jilly Longland, do you think she is a relative of the witch that was burned?"

"I think that is very possible, but I don't know if she realizes that or not. Play it carefully Alana. And keep me informed of any unusual activity."

"I will," Alana affirmed. "I look forward to solving this mystery."

"Good, go and pack what you need and do take some of the bed linen and towels with you. Please be circumspect Alana. I don't want to have to rectify any more of your silly indulgencies. Keep me informed on what you find."

"I will, my queen," Jilly said but under her breath she said, "Will I ever life down my indiscretion?"

"You know that I care about you, Alana, do this for me and all is forgiven."

Her Royal Highness Emelia Rey was a mixture of regal pretension and a little girl who has been given too far many birthday presents.
She was a little bit spoilt but she still cared deeply about her subjects.
"I am looking forward to the challenge," Alana said. "I will keep you informed, as to what is happening in the village."
"That is what I expect, Goodbye and Blessed Be," The Queen said. "And Alana, do try to keep out of trouble."
"I will your majesty. Goodbye and Blessed Be."

Chapter three

Little Barnstead March 1959

Little Barnstead is a small hamlet tucked away in a valley and off the beaten track, and its history went back hundreds of years. In the mid twentieth century it was a village of pretty cottages of little terrace houses, painted white and with umpteen hanging baskets of begonias and hanging ivy.

The village green, where the children gathered and the men played cricket on the weekends, was neat and tidy. But at its centre was a small wood and in the middle of it a large flat stone, often called the Altar Stone or the Witch's Stone.

Alana had been told about the Altar Stone on the village green and was keen to investigate, this historic place.

"What is the story behind this Altar Stone?" Alana asked Wanda as they were working their way through the list of stock that Alana would take over.

"Well, what is not obvious is that in the center of the village green there is clearing surrounded by four large oak trees and some horethorn, there is an ancient flat boulder," Wanda related. "It has always been known as the Altar Stone, it is about fifteen feet across, and on the side of it is engraved the names of all the May Queens going back to the 16th century."

"How lovely," Alana said.

"Yes, it's a beautiful spot. The oaks all have mistletoe growing in their branches. And is still a peaceful place; you can hear the bird's singing and the far-off sounds of people or cars going about the daily life. But sometimes the area seems to stand still and has an aura of dark magic about it. Some people believe that if they touch the Altar Stone, they will remember their youth and have feelings aroused that could become disturbing. People rarely go to this area after dark," Wanda said. "It is said that one could see the ghost of the last May Queen and see how she came to such a tragic end," Wanda continued. "Children avoid the stone but as they became older, boys and girls will gather there and, and I believe that many a first tentative kiss is witnessed by the Altar stone."

"Really?" I must go and visit it." Alana said.

"There is no doubt that late at night some illicit affairs took place on the stone, as lust overcame reason. Because in the past some life changing events happened on that stone, that is hidden by a hand full of trees," Wanda said. "It seems to have chilly magnetism for young lovers or people up to no good."

"Has there been any supernatural activity there in recent years."

"There are rumors, but I don't really know. A young girl, the May Queen, was found dead there five years ago," Wanda said, "there was a lot of speculation at the time, but the case was never conclusive as to how and why she died. But we have not had a May Day celebration held in the village since then."

"Heavens," Alana exclaimed. "I have heard about some of the strange things that are happening here. Have you witnessed any of them?"

"Yes, I have. There have been strange weather events, and plagues of mice. Some people have reported seeing an old woman on the village green at night. She has scared a lot of people as apparently; she rushes at you screaming obscenities and then disappears into an evil smelling mist. And the manor house belonging to old Lady

Jane is said to be haunted, by a former maid that was killed."

"How terrible," Alana said. "I can see that there something more going on here than would normally in a sleepy Devon village."

"I am sure you will get to the bottom of it," Wanda said. "But I need to go somewhere a bit more tranquil, for my final years."

"I can certainly understand that, thank you for staying to ease me in to the running of the shop."

"If think that is the least, I can do Alana. I am sure you will like it in the village and I hope you can find out what is causing these disturbances. "

"I will certainly try," Alana said. "I will give you a call and let you know how things turn out."

"That would be great," Wanda said dusting off her hands and pushing a large box file back on the table. "Well, I think you have everything you need now. I will be off to Cornwall."

"Thank you very much you have been very helpful." Wanda said, taking Wanda's hand. "I hope you enjoy your retirement, Wanda." They both looked up at the clear blue sky. "Nice day."

"It is," Wanda said. "Be sure to call me if there are any queries."

Alana watched as Wanda drove off, and then glanced over at the village green. There were a handful of children playing ball, but otherwise it looked tranquil. She could just make out the small stand of trees, then a dark cloud hung over them for a moment.

Alana shuddered, then sun broke through again. "Don't start getting jumpy," Alana told herself. "Got to keep a level head."

Chapter four

After taking over the gift shop from Wanda, Alana added palm readings and tarot cards to the services offered to village people. Her name spread quickly through the wiccan community and people came from far away to see her and often left with a perplexed expression of their faces.

"How did she know that?" one well-dressed lady asked her companion as they returned outside intending to climb back into their car.

"I bought some lovely crystals did you see?" Meggie exclaimed, but Lady Jane Frost Green was not listening. "And she told me all about Derek, how did she know?" Lady Jane Frost said, "do you really think that she was able to talk to my son, and she asked him what we should do with the east field, you know the one where the animals don't like to go. How did she know about that?"

Meggie helped her mother-in-law back into the car.

"Yes, Jane, my Peter used to say that its cursed," Meggie replied.

Meggie shrugged as she got her mother-in-law settled and struggled to get up beside her. "I know it's nonsense, but the people here are very superstitious."

"My son was full of very silly ideas, Meggie, did we get the bread?"

"Yes, and some nice ham for a sandwich for tea." Meggie replied and then she noticed a tall, pretty woman leaving the dress shop, she had a package under her arm. "Look there goes Brenda Noakes the new reverend's wife, I wonder what she has purchased."

As Meggie stood watching, the shopkeeper put a notice up in the window, I wonder what that is about," Meggie said.

"Nothing good, we will have a look tomorrow, let's get home I am feeling very tired," said Lady Jane, brushing off her jacket, as if it was contaminated, "I feel a bit exposed when we go to see Alana, she just has that effect on me. Its draining."

"She is very odd, and I always feel that she can see right through me." Meggie said, as she started the old Bentley up and headed for home. The old Frost estate was on the edge of the village, just a few minutes' drive away from the main Road.

"Perhaps we will drive into town tomorrow and get some provisions in Waitrose, what do you think Meggie?"

"Great idea," she replied. "It is good to get out of the village now and again."

Little Barnstead had more women than men residents, many soldiers did not come home from the war, husbands, brothers, and sons. There were many in the village who bemoaned this dearth of male company and others that took advantage of this anomaly. One such was the local handy man, Andy, did not find it hard to find lots of little jobs that needed doing around the village, and he also gave good service to those in the know.

Andy was washing his van when he noticed the new Vicars wife leaving the vicarage and decided to introduce himself. She appeared to be going for a walk with her dog.

"Hallo," he said. "I am Andy, I live opposite you."

"Pleased to meet you," she replied. "My name is Brenda, my husband is Jim, Jim Noakes. Oh, and this is Terry."

"Andy Fitts, at your service. How are you settling in?" he asked leaning over to pat Terry on the head, but Terry barked and pulled away from Andy.

"Fine, just getting used to things, you know." Brenda said. "Sorry about Terry he is a bit protective. I think it's the move, he not sure of the territory yet, it makes him a bit jumpy."

"No problem, I am sure he will get to know me. Well, if I can help with anything just let me know. I live opposite you at number four."

"I'll do that," Brenda replied. "Well, I had better be getting on."

"Bye-bye," Andy said watching as Brenda disappeared down the path and onto the green. "Well, she seems nice and is extremely good looking," Andy said to himself.

Andy was about 5ft 9in, he was wiry and fit, with curly brown hair, and twinkling blue eyes that seemed to be merry and convey a message to the lonely ladies of the town. Andy did not go to church, and he often worked on Sundays, in fact he would work any time of day or night, whenever his services were required. He got around on an old Norton motor bike, which was very noisy, he was not exactly discreet in his movements. That bike could often be seen outside certain houses in the village at all times of day and night. He also had a little white van which he used to do his legitimate work. It had the company name 'Odd jobs.' and telephone number on the side.

"Brenda, wife of the new clergy," Mike said, "That will be interesting. She's a stunner."

Chapter five

Alana Withers was not especially pretty, except at times she would look irresistible for a moment, ideal qualifications for the proprietress of the gift shop. She was able to manipulate people, if she wanted them to notice her, they would but, if she did not want to be seen she could walk naked down the street and nobody would even notice her. Her power was considerable, but it was contained, she was there to look after the people in the village. Something in the village was going very wrong, and she was there to find out what it was.

It was a week after the shop had been re-opened and a few villages had come in, more out of curiosity than anything else. But Alana had managed to sell everyone something and make them feel welcome, and Lady Jane had popped in twice now and had a Tarot reading.

"She is at the centre of this unusually activity. I can feel it. There is deep and abiding melancholy in that family." Alana said to herself as she tidied away the tarot deck of cards. "I have to investigate that family. There seem to be no menfolk, just this grandson that is working away from home."

Alana smoothed down her long purple skirt and her multi colored shirt that seemed to have flashes of gold and silver in it, as if it had a life of its own. Alana's hair was long and black, tied pack with a purple ribbon, her eyes where green and at times they seemed to flash like emeralds, and then again, they were soft and understanding. Everybody saw her differently that was her skill, she could glamour herself to be whatever was needed.

"More customers will come when word gets around," Alana

mumbled to herself as she tidied up in the shop.

The ladies of the village soon found that they could talk to Alana. They somehow seem to tell her all their secrets and Alana knew who was unhappy in their marriage and who was having an affair and many other secrets. She had a way of sensing their fears, desires, and gaining their confidences.

Children were her nemesis, they sometimes seemed to see through her disguises and although they feared her, but if they were in groups, they became the taunting imps that she detested so much.

She would smile at them and say, "Good morning children," and then mutter to herself as she drew close to them, mumbling under her breath, to freak them out. They sometimes saw her as a beautiful young woman and other times as an ugly old hag. She scared them, and mostly they kept their distance from her and her shop.

"I long to turn them all into toads or divulge all their secrets but I have to help them, that is my penance, and I can't see any way out of it, without upsetting the Queen," she said to herself. "I could have been sent to a much worse place, a war zone, of a plague land."

Witch Queen Emelia Rey did not take failure lightly. So, Alana tried to keep her venomous remarks to herself and do her job as best she could. Even if it was tiresome and dull, at the moment. She had to discover who had re-awakened the curse. It was her lot, to teach her not to do magic for her own gain, but for the good of others, but she did not have to like it.

The village green, where the children gathered and the men played cricket on the weekends, was neat and tidy. A grassed area with a central thicket with an assortment of trees. But at its center was a large flat stone, often called the Altar Stone or the Witch's Stone. This year there was an abundance of daffodils basking in the early afternoon sunshine. But it was still cold in early April this year, 1959, so there were not many people out on the streets as yet, except a hardy trio of children.

Brian Travas was eight years old and a very outgoing child, his older sister Sofie and little sister Kate were less volatile.

"Let's go and see the old Altar Stone," Brian said.

"I don't want to. It scares me," Little Kate replied.

"Oh. Don't be a scaredy cat, you up for it Sofie?"

"I don't know Brian. It is a bit creepy."

"I despair that I have such a pair of sissy sisters. Come on it will be fun. There is nothing there except an old stone."

"The Alter Stone has all the May Queens names carved on it," Sofie said. "That's romantic. Or it was until Janice died."

"What happened to Janice? Tina Spaiden always seems so sad." Kate looked up enquiringly at her big sister.

"We don't really know Kate. She was found dead on the Altar stone on the morning after the May Day festival, they never really found out what had happened."

"I heard that she was drunk and choked on her own vomit," Brian said. "Maybe her ghost is still there."

"Oh, how horrid," Kate remarked. "I don't want to go there."

"Brian. Be careful what you say. We don't want to upset Kate, do we?" Kate was a pretty child with curly auburn hair like her mother her siblings were dark haired. Their older brother Alfie was away at university.

"Sorry Kate. I am sure it was just a nasty accident." Brian turned away and muttered. "I expect the witch got her."

Kate heard what her brother said, and started to cry. "I don't want to meet the witch," she sobbed.

"Brian!" Sofie said. "Kate don't worry why don't we go and we pick some daffodils and take them home for mum?"

"Or we could pick some flowers for Tina," Kate said. "She is so nice and I think she would like them."

"Yes, we could do that. Tina is helping me to make a new dress for the school graduation dance."

Brian pulled a face and turned away. He looked out over the Village Green towards the stand of trees that hid the Altar Stone. He stilled himself for a moment scowling in disgust at his sister's timidity and talk of party dresses. Then he thought that he could see a figure far away and going into the trees.

"Why don't we pick some flowers for Janice and put them on the stone," he said enticingly he was intrigued at who else might be out there near the clearing on this cool spring day.

"Well, I suppose we could. It would be a nice gesture and we could tell Tina that we have done it for her daughter when we go to give her some flowers."

Kate could see the romantic ideal of that, but she was still a little afraid to go to the old stone. "I don't know Brian. What about the ghost?"

"Don't be a baby there are no such things as ghosts. Surely you know that."

"But my friend Genny saw it and so did her mother, only last week. She said it was a woman in old fashioned clothes. Her hair was all wild and her eyes were red and she was shouting at them, and then she disappeared. Genny was terrified, and so was her mum."

"What rot," Brian said. "Everybody knows that Genny's mum likes a drop of gin and Genny is sent to the pub to take her home. Mrs Fordarm was probably drunk. They imagined it."

"Do you really think so," Kate asked.

"Off course I do, Kate. Come on it will be fun and we can get lots of lovely flowers for mum too."

Brian started to pick some daffodils and then headed off towards the centre of the Village Green. Slowly the girls followed, each gathering an arm full of Daffodils on the way.

"I don't like this," Sofie said, but she trailed after her brother and sister.

As they progressed across the grass. The sun was shining brightly, but gradually some dark clouds were blowing in from the east. Sofie looked up and noticed the change in the sky. "I think it is going to rain, we should go back."

"Don't be silly," Brian said and increased his pace towards the stand of trees. His eyes were glazed and he just continued on, his sisters reluctantly following behind him. When he headed the edge of the large oaks he turned and looked back at his sisters. "What are you waiting for he said. "I am going in."

Kate did not see his eyes and followed behind Brian into the shade.

"Stop," yelled Sofie. "Please stop." But they did not hear her and plunged into the relative darkness of the clearing. Sofie stopped and looked up at the sky that was now dark with black heavy clouds. "It's going to rain we must go back," she yelled but they did not hear her.

Sofie paused for a moment undecided of what to do then she followed her siblings into the shade of the trees and towards the center or the clearing. The large flat stone caught the las few rays of sunshine before it turned dark as the black clouds dominated the afternoon sky.

"Put the flowers on the stone Kate," Brian said. "Here let me help you. It is a bit high." Brian lifted Kate up so she could place a huge brunch of Daffodils on to the Altar Stone. This was the sight Sofie saw when she stumbled into the clearing.

"Oh, how lovely," she murmured. Kate turned and her eyes went wide, Brian was climbing up on the stone, but then he too turned towards Sofie.

"What?" Sofie said, shocked by the look in the children's eyes.

Then there was a flash of lightning that seemed to come down near the children on the stone. A misty female figure materialized and flew across the clearing, landing on the altar stone behind

Kate and Brian.

"No," Sofie screamed, "Come away. Please come away."

A voice permeated the clearing, and the light dimmed.

"Thank you, children," a spine-chilling female voice said. "Now be gone."

All three children froze and Kate started to whimper, but they did not move, it was as if they were frozen in place.

"BE GONE FROM THIS PLACE," the un -natural voice boomed and then there was another bright flash of lightning and the heavens opened. Rain fell hard and violent in the clearing, and the children were soaked within minutes. The ghostly figure turned into a spray of mist and flew off above their heads. Sofie instantly came back to herself, dropping the flowers she grabbed Kate and ran. Brian not far behind her. They exited the shelter of trees and ran across the village green to safety. Kate was crying and shaking with terror. Sofie stumbled on the wet grass and nearly fell. Brian had also bolted and was just behind the girls, he put out an arm to steady them.

"Come on Sofie, let's get away from here," he yelled. Another bright flash of lightning flashed across the sky, followed seconds later by thunder. But the downpour seemed to be lessoning in strength, but by now the trio were soaked to the skin.

When they reached to road, they all stopped. Sofie put Kate down and she stopped crying, but hung on to Sofie's' hand.

"What just happened?" Brian said.

"I don't know Sofie answered, "But, I think we had better go home we are all dripping wet and Kate is very upset."

The rain was definitely less violent now and by the time they got home it was sunny again. Mrs Tavis rushed out of the house to meet them as they approached the Gate House.

"Where were you?" their mother asked, as she wrapped the children in towels.

Brian caught Sofie's eye and she shook her head. "Don't say anything she mouthed at him. She will only worry."

"We saw a lady in the woods and we picked daffodils. Then it rained," Kate said and then she looked down into the hand at the last two bedraggled daffodils and handed them to her mum. "For you," she said.

"Well, thank you," Mrs Travis said. She looked up at the two older children, but they had made their faces blank and offered no other explanation.

"You know you shouldn't really pick the flowers on the village green they are for everybody to enjoy."

"We won't do it again," Sofie said. "Will we Brian?"

"No Sofie, I don't think we will. Sorry mum. I am going up to get dry. Is tea ready?"

"Give me ten minutes to change Kate and finish off."

Mr Travis looked expectantly at Sophie and then turned to carry Kate up to change her clothes. As she turned to go upstairs, she looked back at her daughter. "Do you have anything else to say Sofie?"

"No mum, I have nothing to add."

"But you are shivering."

"I'm okay mum, but I am cold," she said. "I need to change my clothes."

But Sofie was really shaken, she never felt at ease where the Alter Stone dominated the little glade. She remembered Janice, who had been a friend of her brother Alfie, and had died so suddenly and she missed her.

'That awful place. It always makes me feel vulnerable,' Sofie thought to herself. 'Why did Brian always have to push it and why did Little Kate always have to have to follow him?'

Suddenly feeling sick Sofie ran to the bathroom. She dry heaved and her stomach rumbled, but nothing came up, tears ran down her cheeks. 'Why are little boys such monsters.'

"You okay up there, Sofie?" Molly called. "Teas ready."

"I am fine mum, be right down. I just want to change my clothes. I am soaked through."

"Okay Sofie, it's on the table. So don't be too long."

Sofie wiped her face with a flannel and combed back her hair. Took a comfy old jumper and bottoms out of the wardrobe. She plastered smile on her face and descended the stair, but she was feeling far from happy.

'Something is going very wrong in this village' she said to herself. 'I know it.'

Chapter six

The Longland sisters had lived together for their entire lives. Neither had married, but Jilly had had a succession of lovers, some young enough to be her children. The latest being the handy man Andy who was twenty years younger than Jilly.

Where Anne was all lard lines and austerity, Jilly was voluptuous and wore colorful clothes and bright silk scarves. When she was working at her the sculptures, she draped a huge overall over her garb and her long curly grey hair was tied back in a ponytail, from which it soon escaped.

"Well, my lovelies," she said as she regarded her latest creations. "I think you will bring me luck."

She would talk to her statues as if they were her children.

And she was never happier than when she was up to her elbows in clay and was very pleased with her latest figures of a huge breasted woman not unlike the Venus of Willendorf that were found in Austria in the early twentieth century.

"You are coming along nicely," she would say. "Bigger boobs, you say, well if, you are sure."

She talked to her statues, because she rarely had a word of conversation from her sister.

Sometimes the sisters did not speak to each other for weeks on end, they kept to their own part of the house. Jilly to her studio and Anne to the front living room or parlour as she called it.

They had a housekeeper, Molly Travas, that came in every morning except Sunday, she would layout the breakfast things and do a bit of cleaning leave them something to make for lunch and leave.

The sisters mainly communicated with each other via Molly or left notes on the kitchen table for each other. Molly was just leaving when Anne cornered her in the kitchen.

"Are you going to the meeting on Friday?" she asked.

"Yes, Bert and I will be there and the kids too, it could be a good thing for the village. But I think it should be a May Day celebration. It is only three weeks to Easter; it is not enough time to…"

"Well, yes if it is done right, none of that pagan rubbish and no May Queen." Anne interrupted.

"I don't think anyone is going to want a May Queen after…"

"Yes, I agree, and we must also remember to emphasize the religious nature of the season, Easter would be better." Anne said crossing her arms over her chest.

"But if we decide on a May Day, we will have to do some of the traditional May features, like …" Molly started to say but was interrupted by Anne.

"I think it would be better to have a ceremony at Easter, one of devotion and religious study."

"But that would not be much fun for the youngsters, now, would it?"

"Exactly my point, kids today…"

Molly cut in on again at this point. "I have to get home and have lunch before I go over to Lady Jane. I must leave now."

Molly moved towards the door, but Anne had not finished yet.

"Will you support me in this?" Anne asked. "A traditional, religious celebration?"

"I will talk it over with Bert," she said making her escape.

"Tiresome bloody women," Molly muttered under her breath as she hurried home. "She should lighten up bit."

Chapter seven

Molly Travas was a round cheerful women, with curly auburn hair, her husband Bert was the grounds man in the nearby stately house, where Lady Jane Frost lived with her daughter in law.

Molly had four children and three of them lived with her in the Old Gate House. Molly also did a bit of cleaning in the afternoons for Lady Jane and Meggie up at Frost House.

The children aged between eight and twenty-one, two of them went to the local school, they all had the run of the grounds at Frost House, as long as they kept out of the way of Lady Jane.

Molly liked to have a chat and cup of tea with Meggie and would regale her with stories of what the two Longland sisters got up to.

"They are a rum pair, so they are," Molly said, "two people could not be more different."

"Yes, chalk and cheese," Meggie said. "I have never seen them together, it is very strange for sisters to be so extreme, don't you think?"

"My girls are very different, my Sofie and Kate, there is only eight years between them but it might as well be a chasm. Kate is so studious and sensible whereas Sofie, well I don't think she has a bit of common-sense, once she discovered boys that was it, nothing else mattered." Molly sighed. "She has starting work in the dress shop with Tina now that she left school. We are hoping that she will learn a trade. Tina is already showing her how to make things and do alterations and look after the clothes. I think it will be a good for her. And she will be bringing in a little bit of money, that will help," Molly paused. "Your Peter is working away in Bristol, is he coming home for Easter?"

"Yes, I think so. Isn't your Alfie away at university?" Meggie asked, you must miss him?" Meggie looked away, distracted for a moment, as if watching something go past the window.

"Did you see that?" Molly asked.

"No what?" Meggie said looking out the window.

"It's nothing, just a shadow. Yes, Alfie is up in London. Have you heard from Peter lately?" Molly enquired, "You must miss him."

"I do, but he is working hard, and he is coming down from Bristol to stay for a week after Easter, that will be good." Meggie looked up at Molly and smiled. "We will be glad to see him."

"He is an engineer, what is he working on?"

"I am not sure some new transport link, I think, he said that he will be coming to live nearer to us in a few months as it develops."

"Are you going to the meeting about the Easter Fare on Friday?"

Yes," Meggie said. "But don't you think if is a bit late notice for Easter, it would be better for May Day, like we used to do years ago, and the weather will be better."

"I agree. That's a good idea, we should try to get back to normal," Molly paused. "But people don't forget, and it was such an upset, Janice was such a lovely girl, but it's been five years, time to get back to normal?"

Meggie shrugged. "We can suggest May Day and see what response we get. Like you said maybe it is time to move on."

"Agreed, but now, I must get back to work or Lady Jane will be giving me the sack." Molly cleared away the tea things and started to clean the aga, but her mind was still on the tragic events that fatal May Day eve some five years ago.

Molly's husband was a quiet unassuming man, who just got on with things, he loved the outdoors and working with nature. He could be seen, whatever the weather, mending fences, of planting, or looking after the livestock. Lady Jane did not have a big holding, and it barely made any money, she left the running and decisions mostly to Bert, and he liked it that way, he was a man that liked a quiet life.

He got on well with the people in the village, especially David Potts who owned an upholstery shop that sold a bit of furniture and odd bits of bric-a-brac, they did house clearances, he sold on anything he could make a bit on in the shop.

In fact, Bert had taken his son, Brian, into the village and was talking to David about buying some new furniture, he wanted a wall unit or dresser where they could put the good china. He was hoping that David might have something suitable as a birthday present for Molly.

"I might have something you would like," David said. "I have just done a house clearance over in Moeston, and I believe there is a nice wall unit, that would do for you. I have not properly sorted through everything yet. I could let you know."

"That would be great, how much would it cost?"

"Oh, I can do you a good deal, it did not cost me much and there are a few pieces that I can sell on for a good price."

"Good, you'll let me know then, her Birthday is 15th May."

"Sure thing, David said. "What do you think about this Easter Fair idea?"

"It would bring back a bit of life to the village, could be a good thing. Bert said. "Get us on the map again, you could do some advertising. I was going to suggest a fruit and veg competition."

"Good idea." At that moment someone came into the shop.

"I'll be off then," Bert said as he and his son made their exit.

Bert and Molly were not paid well, but they had the use of the Gate House and as much of the farm produce as they needed. There were chickens and goats, so eggs and milk were not a problem. Bert even sold some eggs to the local farm market, and that brought in an extra pound of two. Lady Jane liked to have fresh vegetables on the table, and she never minded if Bert sold a few things to augment his salary.

"This Spring Fair might be just what we need to bring some life back to the village," Bert said to his son. "Could be a lot of fun too, what do you think."

"Yes Dad. Mum thinks that a May Fair would be better than Easter. Would we have a May queen?"

"No Brian, I don't think that will happen."

"Why Dad, why don't people talk about what happened at the last May Fair. I have asked mum and she just said, "I will tell you later." But she never does."

"Well, you see Brian, something horrible happened and people don't like to talk about it."

"What?" Brian said.

"Someone died," Bert said, "and that is all I am going to say."

"I know that someone died dad, But…"

"That's it, boy. Enough. And don't you mention to Mum about this wall unit, okay?"

"Our Alfie will be at home soon, it will be good to see him, Bert said, "I hope he is doing well it is costing us enough."

"Yes Dad, it will be nice to have him back. Andy is organizing a cricket match on the green with a team coming over from Illminster."

"Yes, he told me, we had better start getting some practice."

"Harry will be back by then, and possible Lady Janes grandson, Peter, he is good at games."

"That will be a big help," Bert said. "We would be a bit thin on the ground without them."

"Yes dad," Brian said. He could not help but wonder why nobody would tell him what happened on the Alter Stone, he knew it had something evil about it. 'I am old enough to understand what happened. And I have seen the ghost. Haven't I?'

Brian sulked the rest of the way home but cheered up when his mum said we can have fish and chips tonight for a treat.

Chapter eight

The Meeting on Friday night, March 1959

By seven in the evening on Friday night the small hall next to the church was starting to fill with villagers. Brenda Noakes, Father Jim's wife, had arranged for tea and biscuits and some fruit cake for the attendees.

"Are we ready dear?" Jim asked his wife, "plenty of biscuits?"

"Yes, Jim, and tea and coffee, I hope we have enough milk, but I do have some long-life in the cupboard, if we run low."

"Good, good," he replied distractedly.

The vicar almost seemed animated, he wore his dog collar with casual shirt and trousers. Little did the crowd of villages know that he was wearing a lovely lilac Agent Provocateur bra and panties under the sober clothes. Brenda knew, and had to stop herself from sniggering as she passed out cups of tea to the first arrivals, Mr and Mrs Potts from the furniture renovation shop.

"How are you? Have some tea, "Brenda said welcoming them into the hall. "I hope we can count on your support."

'If they knew what I know,' she thought to herself, 'what I have to put up with.' Brenda smiled at the couple.

"I will see you later, "she said.

Meggie arrived with Lady Jane Frost and Father Jim made a beeline for them and planted them in seats at the front of the hall, he was less welcoming when Alana Withers entered with Tina from the dress shop. They seemed to be trying to outdo each other with stunning outfits, more suitable for a wedding than a meeting in the church hall

They were followed by the Longland sisters, Jilly and Anne, who arrived separately Jilly strode in alone and went straight over to talk to Alana Withers. While Anne arrived with the Travis family, Molly, Bert and three children, who took up a row in front of the small stage.

The room was filling up when at seven o'clock Jim called for the meeting to begin.

"Dear villagers," Jim began, "Welcome, I have not had the pleasure of meeting many of you before," he paused, "my wife and I have an idea of organizing a village fair, over Easter…"

Before he could continue, Anne stood up.

"This is a religious holiday is that appropriate?"

Then Meggie said, "Do you think Easter is the right time, it is only three weeks, would not May Day be a better time for a…"

Then there was a general commotion, as several people tried to talk at the same time, before Father Jim brought the meeting back under control.

It was then that Andy Fitts entered and stood at the back of the hall, he leaned against a pillar with his arms folded and surveyed the crowd. Jilly turned and winked at him, much to her sister's chagrin.

"Strumpet, "she muttered under breath, and Molly turned to look at her aghast, then she looked back to towards Father Jim.

A few people had turned and looked at Tina who had gone very pale, and seemed to want to say something, but no sound came out of her mouth.

"Do you think that would be appropriate after what happened four years ago, it might be a bit difficult for Tina," Molly said

"We need to move on," Meggie said. "How would you feel about a traditional May Day celebration Tina?" Meggie turned to face Tina and Molly who were on the seats across from her.

Tina was quiet for a few seconds and then she replied.

"I think that we should move on. I will never forget the death of my daughter, but that is no reason why the village should not have its May Day celebration." She was quiet for second. "I only ask that it is done properly and with respect and does not become a drunken brawl."

"I agree," Meggie said, and smiled at Tina, who nodded and looked down at her hands, where she was twisting the handle of her bag.

"What happened four years ago?" Jim asked. At which point everybody started talking at once. When Jim managed to get everybody's attention again, he said. "Can we have a short break and we will then do a vote for Easter or May Day, there is tea and cakes, we will reconvene in fifteen minutes."

He then turned to his wife and spoke.

"Do you know what they are talking about?" she shrugged and said, "I will find out," and then she went off to talk to Molly, taking her into the small kitchen for privacy.

Molly related the tragic story of the death of Tina's daughter.

"On May Day we always had a pageant and a May Fair and one of the village girls would be crowned as May Queen," Molly began.

"But what happened five years ago," Brenda asked.

"It was terrible, we had a lovely day and Tina's daughter, Janice, was crowned May Queen, she was crowned in the woods on the Altar Stone and it was..." Molly paused.

"But whatever happened?" Brenda asked again.

"Well, the day went well, and a good bit of alcohol was drunk, and the youngsters partied, it all seemed good natured. But the following morning Janice was found dead. She was only eighteen, and the prettiest little thing, the village people were devastated."

"How terrible," Brenda replied. "What happened?"

"We never found out, she had drunk a lot of alcohol and it looked like an accidental death, but she had had sex on the Altar Stone, you know where I mean, the Altar Stone in the clearing?

"My goodness no wonder there is a problem with a ..."

"There was no sign of violence, and it was assumed that she had just passed out and died during the night." Molly interrupted. "But my husband was there when they found her and he said … he said her face was like a grimace, we think she died of shock."

"How dreadful. Did she have a weak heart?"

"No that it the thing … The coroner could find nothing wrong with her heart."

"Did the police ever find out what happened?" Brenda asked.

"No, they never found out what happened, and it was put down to a tragic accidental death. But there are many people in the village who believe that she was murdered. And no one came forward to say that they had been with her on the stone, if you know what I mean…"

Molly and Brenda returned to the main hall, there was a buzz of conversation, but all went quiet as Brenda walked up to the front of the hall and joined her husband.

"What is going on," he asked quietly.

"I will fill you in later," she said. "I suggest we ask for a vote on the Mayday date and ask for ideas, then set up another meeting for next week to discuss details."

And that is what they did.

As people drifted away, talking quietly to each other, Brenda explained to her husband what had happened.

"This is a sinful place, "he muttered. "Why did they have to send us here?"

"You should know," she replied and walked away, leaving him standing there wondering what he had done, to make life so difficult. then he remembered and went into the church to pray.

Jim Noakes was a drab little man with premature greying hair of a sort of dirty looking sandy colour. He had been sent to the village for his sins, he was being punished for his vice. He wore his knees out repenting but could not contain his desires. His wife was standing by him, but at times she could not contain her contemp. If her father had not been a high up official in the church, they would have lost everything, he would have had to leave the church, and he was not qualified to do anything else.

Brenda Noakes, surprised most people when they met her for the first time, she was pretty in an unadorned sort of way. Always cheerful and helpful, with a long languid body and wide shoulders. Some people were amazed that a dull little man like Jim had managed to marry such a lovely girl.

Father Jim's church services were poorly attended, and he did not seem inclined to go around the village trying to drum up an audience.

"He has lost his drive," Brenda told her father.

"Well, he had better find it again. Or that will not be the only thing he loses."

"It's so difficult for me Dad," Brenda said. "I don't have any feelings for him anymore."

"I know girl. But try and hold on a year or so more and then we can see what we can do."

"Okay dad." Brenda looked down at her hands, that were clasped in her lap. But I feel that it is me that is being punished," she said.

Chapter nine

Saturday morning Brenda awoke early and decided to take the dog for a walk. He was a terrier cross with something unknown added. He had the terrier shaped ears, that jumped to alertness at the sound of his lead being taken off the hook in the kitchen.

"Come on boy," Brenda said, and Terry jumped up and down until she managed to get the lead on him. "I need to get out of here for a while."

Brenda was feeling very grumpy, Saturday night Jim had returned to the house after praying in the church for about an hour, he was very agitated. Brenda had given in to his desires and let him sleep in her bed. They did not have sex, he seemed unable to get an erection anymore, but he liked to cuddle up with her, especially if she allowed him to wear one of her flimsy nighties.

"Terry, fancy a nice long walk?" Brenda said addressing her dog.

Terry looked up and wagged his tail and gave a short sharp woof.

Brenda knew that Jim would feel guilty this morning and Brenda wanted to be out of his way for a few hours.

Her feet led her across the village green towards the stand of trees at its center.

"Come on boy we will go and look at this Altar Stone," she said, and Terry looked up at her in agreement.

It was still early morning, just after seven, the sun was still rising, the birds were calling to each other. As she approached the small grove of trees, the air seemed stiller. With the last traces of sunrise still in the sky. She entered the area and saw the flat stone for the first time in the half-light, it cast a shadowy presence.

"Not scary at all," she said. "What do you think Terry?"

Terry did not like the look of it and tried to pull Brenda away.

She had not realized how large it was, at least fifteen feet long and about twelve feet across, the stone had a flat top, in a grey/blue colour, some sort of granite she supposed.

On the front of the stone was a flattened panel with the names of the May Queens going back many hundreds of years, but they stopped five years ago.

'How lovely she thought,' the air was very still, and Brenda suddenly realized that it has gone very quiet.

Terry had stopped pulling and his ears were standing up to attention, as if he was listening to something.

"Do you sense something Terry?" Brenda said.

Then Brenda felt it, a shiver ran down her spine, there was an air of gaiety, and it sounded like children's laughter, but combined to that a malignant presence that seemed to want to smother all the joy. Brenda found it quite disconcerting, and then suddenly it was as if someone or something brushed against her, nearly knocking her into the edge of the stone.

"Is there anybody there?" Brenda asked.

Then Terry started barking loudly. Brenda looked around, but could not see anything. She decided to leave and Terry dragged her away back towards the village green.

As she reached the edge of the trees, she turned and looked back.

There was something, a shape, a shadow, someone standing by the stone, Brenda blinked, and it was gone.

Then Terry urgently pulled her away until they were back in the bright April sunshine once more.

"Well, that was odd," she said to the dog, "You really didn't like it in there did you boy?"

Terry barked three short yaps and pulled on the lead until they were well away from the trees.

When she returned home, she could hear Jim in the bathroom, so she put the kettle on for tea and started getting the breakfast ready.

"I don't think we will tell Jim about that," she said giving Terry's ears a rub. "It will only make him more jittery."

Terry barked once and went to drink some water from his bowl. Then he looked up at Brenda, as if in agreement and retreated to his basket.

When Jim came down a few minutes later, he was dressed in his priestly shirt and collar.

"Good morning, Brenda. I have been thinking that if we are going to have this May Fair, we must start to make a list of possible attractions, don't you think? I have started work on a leaflet, maybe you could take some to put up in the village, and I will contact the local paper."

Brenda nodded and turned to the frying pan. "Do you want eggs and bacon?" she asked.

"Yes please," he replied, his head already bowed over a notebook writing a list of things they needed to do.

"I will remind the congregation in church tomorrow, about the May Day Fair and ask for ideas for next week."

'All six of them,' Brenda thought to herself.

After making the breakfast Brenda cradled her cup of tea in her hands and settled down in a kitchen chair and she watched her husband, 'this is a strange place' she thought,' is this my life now?'

Andy had spent the night with Jilly, they were lovers, but they were also good friends, and had an enduring friendship. As he was arriving home, he spotted Brenda coming back with her dog from a walk. He pulled up outside his little house, she did not seem to notice him, so he just stood and watched her, thinking that she was a fine-looking woman if only she made a bit more of herself.

'I suppose if you are married to a stuffy old Vicar,' Andy thought with a grin, 'you don't really need to glam yourself up. I wouldn't mind getting to know her better,' he thought, 'perhaps I could volunteer to do something for this May Fair, I could get into her good books, and who knows?'

Andy had been in the army during the war. He never saw much action, but made himself very useful and qualified as a carpenter. He was now a good general fix it man.

After he was de-mobbed, he got some work as a painter and decorator, and first came to the village to do some work for Lady Jane Frost. She had lost her son, Derek, in the war, and was now living with her daughter-in-law, Meggie.

He started doing up some of the rooms, and found he enjoyed being his own boss and gradually more work came his way, he liked the village and when a small cottage came up for sale, he bought it.

He met Jilly in the gift shop in the village when he was visiting to buy some candles. The gift shop, Pandoras Box, then run by Wanda, was stocked with scented candles and incense, and some esoteric items. A large collection of books and magical paraphernalia. Statues of the green man, and other subjects made by Jilly, the local sculptress, plus crystals and charms. The store certainly attracted quite a few diverse customers, sidling in and out, at all hours.

While Wanda was wrapping his purchase, Andy turned towards Jilly.

"Hallo," Andy said, I don't think we have met?"

"No, my name is Jilly. Jilly Longland, how do you do?" she asked. Jilly appraised him and she liked what she saw.

"I do very well," he replied with a smile, he had been quite taken by this striking looking woman.

"Jilly wants some building work done," Wanda had said, as she looked on with an amused look in her eyes.

"Really," Andy said, "tell me more."

"I want some work done in my studio, a larger window and insulation and then some decorating in the house," Jilly said. "Would you be interested?"

"Yes, how urgent is it?" Andy enquired. "I am bit busy this week, but I am free after that."

"It is not very urgent." Jilly said. "Can you give me a quote?"

"Yes, can I pop around to see what is needed?" Andy asked.

"Yes please, we are the last house at the end of Green Lane, number 8. Tomorrow late afternoon okay for you?"

"That would be fine," he replied.

They had hit it off right away and had been friends and part time lovers ever since. They had the same sense of humor and loved to wind up Jilly's pious older sister Anne, and it was very easy to get her riled, as she seemed continually on the edge of reason these days, and it took very little to get her off on one of her tirades.

"You will never believe what it is like in that house, "Andy said to Sheila Potts, he had popped into the furniture and upholstery shop to look at a little cupboard he had seen in the window.

"They live in completely different parts of the house; and rarely meet in the kitchen. The atmosphere is so hostile when Anne is around. I don't think she is quite right in the head if you know what I mean."

"I don't know her well, seen her at church of course, but we have never really spoken apart from a quick hallo."

"Yes, she is very religious, constantly quoting the bible and the names she calls Jilly, it's something terrible." Andy shrugged. "Not a religious man myself, but we have to respect the right to choose for themselves, don't we?"

"Yes, I suppose we do, now what is it you want, the little wooden cupboard in the window, would twenty quid be alright? You can take it away with you now."

"That would be great," Andy said, and pulled the money from his pocket while Sheila got the little chest of drawers from the window for him.

"Thanks Sheila be seeing you.

"My pleasure," Sheila replied.

"Are you okay with this Easter Fair, or May Fair or whatever they are going to call it?"

"Yes Andy. I am fine with it. The village needs to get some of its life and character back. Everything seems very charged at the moment." Sheila smiled. "Anyway, it could be good for business."

Chapter ten

The Longland sisters had never really got on, but as they were left the house jointly by their parents, they muddled along, living together, but never really communicating.

Anne did talk to her dead fiancé, and to other people no one could see. Many people thought that she was crazy or a bit affected.

"What would you do my heart?" she asked, addressing the second comfy chair in her parlor, it is a right state of affair, don't you think? That Andy was over again last night with Jilly. I could hear them laughing and getting up to God knows what," Anne made the sign of the cross in the air. "She is a right strumpet, and no mistake. I know what mischief she got up to the in the war with those American soldiers. Let the devil take them both, that's what I say."

Off course no one answered her. "Damn them, and damn you for leaving me," she shouted, and the window rattled, and it seemed to go very dark for a moment. Outside in the back garden three brown spotted toads hopped up the garden path and settled on the doorstep and the sky darkened as if threatening a storm.

"Men," she shrieked. "Always trouble. Damn them all."

Anne lost her fiancé in the war and had never really got over it, she seemed to blame him for deserting her, and now she seemed to demonize all men, as feckless and selfish.

When she heard that he had died, she cut off her long curly auburn hair and only wore old clothes that her mother had left. Now at the age of sixty-three she was going grey and her short-cropped hair, was like a helmet, badly cut and ugly.

"Why does Jilly have it all when I have lost everything."

Anne's anger and resentment left a miasma of feeling wherever she went, and she seemed to resent anyone for being happy, or prettier or brighter than herself. She had been a teacher for thirty years, and was a formidable disciplinarian, not liked by her pupils or the other staff at the local school. Her gasping at religion was blinding her to a life of bitterness and anger, which made her very difficult company.

Anne knew little of her antecedents, and certainly; did not know that there had been witches in the family five hundred years ago.

Andy called at the vicarage the following day and was pleased when Brenda opened the door.

She looked at him in confusion at first and then said, "Andy, isn't it?" Terry was barking, but seemed to accept Andy, after a sniff or two at his hand, he plodded off to his basket.

"Yes," he replied. "I want to offer to help with this May Day Fair, can we talk about it and see what I can do?" he reached to give Terry a stroke. "Nice friendly dog what's his name?"

"Terry. Why yes, of course, do come in," Brenda said as she stood aside and let him pass into the hallway. "Let's go into the kitchen it's nice and warm in there and I have just put some coffee on, would you like a scone? I made them yesterday?"

Andy strolled into the kitchen which was large and modern. Brenda followed him, her hand rising to smooth her dark brown hair and then to straighten and tuck in her blouse.

"This is a lovely big room, what a difference to my tiny kitchen," he said. "In fact, my kitchen would fit in here three times."

"Well, when we were sent to this god forsaken place, I insisted on a kitchen utility extension. Oh, I should not have said that, sorry."

"Don't fret on it. I don't have much time for all this god stuff, I have to admit. But I would like to help out at the May Fair, if you let me." Andy paused. "Is your husband in?"

"No, he had to go out, into town for something."

"Well, do you think I can help?" Andy asked, "I have some contacts, that may be of assistance, or if there is any grunt work. I can do that."

"All hands to the deck, as they say," Brenda replied, and for the first time she looked directly at Andy, 'he is a very attractive man' she thought.

Brenda waved her hand towards a chair at the table and turned to prepare the coffee. Her face had flushed, and she was thinking that Andy was hot. It had been a long time since any urges of that nature had affected her composure. By the time she turned with two mugs of coffee she had her emotions under control.

"Would you like a scone or two? I have jam and butter?"

"Well, yes, you are spoiling me," Andy said with a grin.

"I need to use them up, Jim, my husband, does not care for sweet things." Brenda shrugged her shoulders and Andy could sense that this marriage was not a happy one.

"I love sweet things, in moderation of course, got to watch my figure."

Brenda ran her eyes over his slim chest and arms.

"You look in good shape to me," she said and then blushed again.

"I like to keep fit," he said and started to eat the scones, then he looked up at Brenda a twinkle in his eye.

"What can I do for you?" he said, turning his head to the side and looking deep into her eyes, which he noticed were a pale green/blue in colour.

Well," Brenda said flustered by the intimacy that seemed to be growing between them. "I am not sure at the moment, but we were thinking that some of the villagers might like to have a table of wares for sale and I will need some tables for drinks and snacks. Meggie, and Jilly and Anne Longland have suggested making some cakes for sale."

"Anne Longland, I would be careful what I ate from her kitchen," Andy said.

"She is a bit …"

"Sour, I think the word is," and then added, "she could sour milk by looking at it."

"Yes, she is a bit tiresome there's no doubt. Were you here, in the village, when that girl died?" Brenda asked suddenly.

"Yes, it was a terrible time."

"Do you know what happened?"

"I don't, there were many rumors at the time, and some of local boys were under suspicion, but nothing could be proven."

"Poor Tina it must have been horrible for her, this town is …"

"There are certainly a lot of secrets," Andy replied, "It seem that everybody had a skeleton in their cupboard."

"Yes," Brenda said, 'little do they know,' she thought, 'little do they know.'

Andy finished his tea and put the last crumbs from the scones in his mouth. Then he looked up at Brenda, his face seemed to want to ask something else, but then he changed his mind.

"Delicious," he said. "Your husband does not know what he is missing."

"I am glad you could use them up for me," Brenda replied.

"Indeed, I'll be off then," he said standing and closely observing Brenda. "I will find out about trestle tables."

"That's great," Brenda said. "See you soon."

"I will get back to you," he said, with a most disarming smile, his blue eyes dancing in front of her.

As Brenda saw him to the front door he suddenly turned and stood very near, face to face just inches apart. She could smell his aftershave with just the faint smell of perspiration, newly sawn timber, and glue.

"If there is anything else, I can do for you. Let me know." Andy said. "I am just across the road." He winked and was gone, leaving Brenda in a state or turmoil. Get a grip on yourself she thought to herself, returning to the kitchen and starting to clear the table.

"What did you think of him, Terry." The dog raised his head, to look at Brenda, the chewy bone forgotten for a moment, he gave a halfhearted couple of barks before flopping down again, to resume chomping on his toy bone.

"Yes, me too," Brenda said then reached to scratch Terry's ears. "Me too."

It had been some time since Brenda had felt any sexual excitement. But she realized that she was having some very erotic thoughts about Andy.

"I had better watch myself around him," Brenda said to herself.

Chapter eleven

"Have I told you about our family history," Lady Jane said to Meggie one morning.

"A little," Meggie replied, "and Derek also mentioned that the family goes back a long way, he said that it was before the time of Henry the eighth."

"Yes, the Frost family goes back hundreds of years, to a distant ancestor who was a noble man in the time of Henry the eighth. Lord Frost was given the Frost Estate as a gift for helping Henry during the dissolution of the monasteries," Lady Jane said. "Did you know that Anne Boleyn was be-headed and accused of being a witch by Henry's court."

"I knew she was executed. But, no, I did not know that she was accused of witchcraft, how terrible."

"Lord Frost had persecuted many Catholics at the time and his son, David Frost, played a big part in victimizing witches, or hedge women as they were often called," Lady Jane said.

"But most so-called witches were simply herbalists or women who had to make a living, selling cure-alls and herbs, and possible love charms."

"Yes, but it was a time of hatred and mistrust, and the vulnerable were always singled out, because they often stood alone. Witches were killed and their bodies either burned or buried in some field or heath land outside of the town or village."

"Derek told me about the East field, he said that nothing seemed to grow there, and it was a pasture that animals avoided," Meggie said. "He thought that plague victims were buried there."

"We believed that it was a burial site, for burials that were outside the sanctified grounds of the church."

"How ghastly," Meggie said.

"True, even some of my relatives, many died of the plague and other diseased back then. This household has had far too many tragedies, many a boy did not live to see adulthood. Why even, my own brothers died in their prime?"

"How terrible. And my Derek, he died too young. And before we could have any more children," Meggie said sadly.

"It is sad, but you have Peter, he will the take the family line forward. Meggie I am so glad that you have stayed with me," Lady Jane said. "I love you like a daughter. You know that don't you?"

"I do. And I love you Jane," Meggie replied. "It is so interesting to know about the past. I know nothing about my family history."

"Sometimes it is better not to know my dear.

"But surely it is good to know one's history?"

"My ancestor, David Frost, had Alice Park charged with witchcraft and hanged, and her daughter also died, she was burned to death denounced by Gerald Frost." Lady Janes paused. "Maud Park Longland, cursed the Frost family, as she burned. She called out, 'your seed will continue in jeopardy and your menfolk will die badly like weeds in the grass.' This is my gift to you." Lady Jane paused again and looked up at Meggie. "The men of the household never seemed to live very long, and even the ones that survived had tragic lives. They were killed or maimed in war and or by illness." Lady Jane continued. "John Frost himself died only a few months after the death of the witch Maud Park Longland, he succumbed to syphilis and madness, and having lost his mind and jumped off the roof. David had an older brother Gerald, who succeeded the tittle and Frost House, he left behind a wife and three children, two boys and a girl." Lady Jane said.

"How do you know all this?" Meggie asked.

"Lady Elizabeth Frost, David's mother, kept a journal that has been handed down through the family."

"That is amazing, can I see it?"

"Yes, but it is very fragile, and locked away for safety," Lady Jane said. "The women folk of the family were strong, and the generations continued, to the present day. And now it all relies on Peter."

"He will marry and keep the blood line going," Meggie said.

"That is what I pray for, my dear," Lady Jane said. "It would be wonderful to have some great-grandchildren running about the place before I die."

Lady Jane and Peter were the last of the Frost blood line, Jane's two brothers were both deceased, now Lady Jane's only family was her daughter in law Meggie and her grandson Peter.

Wishing to change the subject Meggie asked, what Lady Janes thought about the May Fair.

"I have several ideas, about the May Fair, and have been making some notes, for the next meeting on Friday."

"Really?" Meggie asked. "What do you suggest?"

"How about a flower arranging competition," she suggested.

Meggie was making the breakfast this morning because Molly had asked for the day off to visit someone in the nearby town. "And there could be some stalls of local product and an area showing the history of the village, what do you think?"

Meggie turned from the frying pan where she was cooking some eggs and bacon.

"I think that's a great idea. One egg or two?"

"What the hells that?" Lady Jane screeched and pointed toward the back door.

A large spotted toad had just hopped across the kitchen floor. Meggie quickly opened the door and it hopped out and disappeared into the garden.

"How did that get in here?" Meggie said, looking shocked.

Lady Jane had gone quiet pale and slumped down in her seat.

"Are you okay, "Meggie asked, going over to her mother-in-law who looked as if she was going to faint.

"I am fine," she said, and the colour returned to her face, "I am fine, don't fuss."

Meggie turned back to her cooking and plonked two eggs and some bacon on a plate and put it in front of her mother-in-law.

"There eat that, and I'll get the toast," she said. "There is butter on the table. I will make a fresh pot of tea."

"Shall we go into town and get some shopping," Lady Jane asked, but she still looked a bit shaken. "I need to go to the bank."

"Yes, why not. I want to send a parcel to Peter, he asked for me to send him his best waistcoat and his bow tie for some special dinner or something," Meggie replied. "We will have our breakfast. I will wash up and then get our coats and off we go, but I want to drop that green jacket into Tina on the way, see if she can do something with it, that okay?"

"Yes," Lady Jane said, but as she spoke, she looked towards the back door, a look of fear came over her face.

"What is it?" Meggie said, her gaze echoing that of her mother-in-law.

It's the …" she murmured, "she's gone."

"Who's gone?" Meggie asked.

"Take no notice of me, the toad gave me a shock, that's all."

"Are you sure you want to go out?" Meggie asked. "You look very pale."

Lady Jane nodded and then ate her breakfast; only once more did her eyes go towards the back door. And then she shrugged and continued eating.

Chapter twelve

Molly taking the day off had also left Jilly and Anne to their own devises that morning, and Anne was preparing her breakfast when Jilly entered the kitchen.

"Morning" Jilly said.

"Yes," said Anne, "Do you want some tea?"

Jilly looked at her sister, these had been the first words between them in the last week.

"I have been thinking about this May Fair idea. I could make some of my cakes for sale, what do you think?" Anne asked.

"What a good idea," Jilly replied warily. "I think they would go down very well. I was also thinking about the fair, I might offer to do a stall or something,"

"You not going to be selling your figures, are you?"

"Well, maybe, I mentioned it to Alana and she said that we could do something together," Anne grunted, but Jilly continued, "and Tina wants to make some little gifts, little cloth bags and cushions with lavender, that sort of thing."

"I don't like that woman," Anne said abruptly.

"Who Tina? She's very nice …"

"No, not Tina, the witch." Anne scowled at her sister forgetting the toast until it started to burn, and then hastily she pulled it free of the grill, and grabbing up a knife scraping at the black bits over the sink before putting it down on a plate.

"I don't think she is a witch," Jilly said, "She is just a new age shopkeeper. That's all. She seems very nice."

"The church has a decree that magic is evil because it attempts to appeal to powers beyond those of God. It cannot be permitted. The bible says we must not permit a witch to live." Anne seemed to have gone off into one of her a trance, then she blinked and stared up at Jilly.

"She is evil, I feel it. And you will be condemned, as a harlot, letting that young man stay the night, don't you imagine that I don't know what you get up to, out there in your den of iniquity. Harlot! God will make you pay, heed my words. Acting like a complete trollop, the way you do."

"You're out of your mind," Jilly said grabbing up a slice of toast and spreading it with butter and some chunky marmalade, before getting up and pouring herself a cup of tea from the pot.

"You are living dangerously by not embracing the lord, it will fall on you, wait and see," Anne said, "sleeping with a man nearly half your age, you will go to hell. At least it's a man and not a woman this time."

"What are you talking about?" Jilly asked.

"Did you think I did not know, about your little liaison with the girl in Bristol?" Anne retorted.

"Oh, do shut up, your silly old bag," Jilly said going out the back door, and leaving her sister sitting there mumbling to herself. "I am only fifty-seven, I am not going to live like a nun."

Anne turned her face to the slammed door, gritting her teeth and making a cross with her hands across her chest.

"You will see the way of your sin," She shouted. "You trull, you trollop, how can you be my sister. Let the hail of hell be on your head."

Outside the wind rattled against the window and a shower of hard rain fell crashing on the roof and blowing the blossoms off the trees. Pounding hard against the back door, which flew open and then slammed shut once more.

"Halleluiah, it flows," Anne said as she sat back in her chair poured herself another cup of tea, and then nibbled away at the burnt toast. Her eyes were glazed and malicious as she hummed Onward Christian soldiers to herself.

It remined wet with occasional hail showers, for the reminder of that day and there some were minor floods in the houses near the river.

Chapter thirteen

The Village 1558

There is a lot of tension in the Frost household, when their maid Alice was found to be pregnant by David Frost.

"She is nothing to me," David said, "she tempted me and wedeled her way into my bed, she is a witch and she captivated me with her spells. I renounce her and all her kind."

"Are you making a formal complaint?" Lord Frost asked, "you know where that would lead, she would be killed, if it went to court."

"She will never work again at this house while I am alive. I will not abide to have the conniving woman remain in my sight." David ranted at his father. "I will go to London Town you deal with it."

Lord Frost looked at his son, he knew that David was a womanizer and a rake, and that the poor girl had been his victim, rather than the other way around.

"I will tell you what we will do, the girl will be dismissed and can find her own way, and you will go up to London for a year, and try not to get any more girls pregnant."

"As you say, father," David said and packed his bags and was gone that same day.

David Frost alienated himself with his bad behaviour in London. Falling out with friends and family, gambling then and ravaged with the pox, near insane he was shipped off to a retreat in Tangiers, where he remained for a further two and a half years.

By the time he returned to Devon, he was a weak and bitter man. When he saw that Alice, Park was still in the village, he was furious.

"How can you allow that trull bitch to remain in the village, I don't believe it, living here with her little bastard," David roared. "Get her away, he ranted and raved. "I cannot abide it."

Lord and Lady Frost were worried for their son's sanity.

"What shall we do?" Lady Frost asked, he is not rational, and the sight of that woman and her child drives him deeper into madness."

"I will get her to leave the area," he said, "if we give her some money she can move elsewhere."

But David Frost had other ideas and he went to the local magistrate and made a formal complaint of witchcraft against Alice Park, and she was arrested two days later.

Little Maude was taken in by a Mr and Mrs Longland, while her mother was in jail accused of witchcraft.

Alice was kept awake for days on end walked back and forward day and night, nonstop and constantly questioned.

"You are a witch tell us who is in your coven, who else is in league with the devil, then it will end, just tell us who else is involved."

She was tortured and tormented, had pins stuck into her body, to try to get an admission of witchcraft, which she always denied, until she felt so weak, that she made no sense and was left to rot for several weeks in a fetid cell, with nothing but a crust of bread and a cup of water a day, for sustenance.

"I am not guilty," she told to her jailers, but she never stood a chance not with the son of a rich and powerful family calling for her death.

Alice Park was found guilty in 1558, and they kept her in Exeter County jail until she died at the end of a rope.

The child was just coming up to her forth birthday, and too young to understand what was going on. She had a pretty delicate face and curly auburn hair, just like her mother.

Everybody knew that Maud was the bastard daughter of David Frost, and that he had pursued Alice Park when she was a housemaid in the house, and then shunned her when she fell pregnant. David was the second son of the Lord Frost, poor Alice was sacked and vilified by the Frost family. For three years she made a meager living selling herbs and doing sewing and washing for the local residents. Most people felt sorry for her, and her child, but could not risk upsetting Lard Frost and his family, who more of less owned the village, so when Alice was accused of witchcraft, nobody came forward to defend her.

"We will take on the child," Johan Longland said. "I can't see her go to the poor house. This is not her fault."

Johan Longland was the grounds man on the Frost estate and he and his wife Jean defied the Frost family when that said that they were going to take the little girl into their family. There was protest at first, but the wife of the lord and the older son Gerald stepped in and persuaded Lord Frost that it was the right thing to do.

"We cannot, be responsible for an innocent child's destitution and demise, she is not the guilty one, "Lady Frost said. "Let her stay with the Longlands's she will be safe there."

"I see no harm," Gerald said, "but she must not be told of her parentage."

"I agree," said Lord Frost, "let that be an end to it."

Lady Frost felt that it was the least they could do for the poor motherless girl. After Alice was executed Lady Frost often visited the girl, who was really her granddaughter, and she became very fond of her.

"What a pretty child," she said, one day when she visited the Longland cottage. "Such lovely hair. Her mother was fair if I remember rightly."

"Yes," said Jean, who had been very wary of the lady of the big house, but now welcomed her visits because she would often bring with her some tasty food or a little something for the child, such as a new little coat or some underwear, which was very helpful as the Longlands who were not well off. Working for the gentry never made anybody rich.

As Maud learned to speak, she called Mrs Longland mother and Lady Frost, auntie, not knowing until much later that she was related to the Frost household and that Lady Frost was in fact her grandma.

"She looks as if she is in another world," Lady Frost said one day, when she was playing with the girl. Maud seemed far away, and appeared to be seeing things or people that no one else could see.

"Just look at that robin, he has no fear," Lady Frost said, as Maud fed the little bird from her own hand.

"Yes, I have seen frogs and toads climb out of the pond and come to be near her, and birds and animals do not seem to fear the girl. One day I even saw a deer come to the garden and Maud was able to stroke it."

"How wonderful," Lady Frost said. "You love her then? With her faraway wistful ways?"

"Indeed, she's a little dreamer, but no trouble to look after. We are so very fond of her," Jean said, "we love her very much."

"As I do too, I wish things had been different," Lady Jane said, "my son David is very ill now, we think he will die."

"But that is terrible, David was, well … I don't know what to say Lady Frost. It is never easy to lose someone, even if…"

"Even if he deserved it, is that what you mean to say?

"No, my lady, I would never…"

"But it is true none the less," Lady Frost said," he is not a good man." Lady Frost looked sadly at her friend and wiped away a tear.

The two ladies of very different births sat quietly together and watched the pretty curly headed child as she appeared to be playing with sunbeams. Not long after David Frost died, he was crazed, weak and riddled with syphilis he jumped off the roof into the paved pathway, he died instantly. His mother lived on another eight years and then she too died, but peacefully in her bed. But Lady Frost's legacy changed the life of little Maud, the child that should have been her grandchild.

Chapter fourteen

The village 1959

In the village of Little Barnstead there were a few little shops, a small super market and post office, a dress shop that did dressmaking and some repairs and had some dry-cleaning and washing facilities, this was run by Tina, a stately lady with very pretty curly blond hair, she had lived in the village for about thirty years.

"Tina could manage an entire family's outfits for a wedding or special occasion, should it arise," Molly once told Meggie. "You can rely on her for alterations, she is very conscientious."

"Thanks Molly," Meggie said.

Meggie had asked Molly if she would recommend Tina, because there were a few sewing jobs that she needed doing. Meggie was very practical but not good at that sort of thing.

"Can you alter this jacket for me? it is a bit tight round the middle," Meggie asked. "It is old, but I like the colour."

"Yes, Tina said, picking up the jacket and looking at the inside tucks and seams. "I can let out these tucks and move the buttons over, should do the trick. Is it okay over the shoulders?"

"Yes, it is just the middle, put on a few pounds around the waist since I last wore it," Meggie said.

"Haven't we all," Tina replied, picking up a small pair of scissors and starting to unpick one of the darts.

The village never knew much about Tina except that she was a widow and very helpful, and that she had had two children. Her son Harry who was away at university, and her daughter who was dead, the victim of that fateful night of May. Janice had died, as May Queen, under very suspicious circumstances. Tina kept very to herself these days, but she always seemed to be there for others in need.

"You can pick the jacket up in a couple of days is that okay, it won't take me long," Tina said. "I will get the jacket steam-cleaned as well take all the creases out."

"That's great, I will see you on Friday then," Meggie said, "are you going to the meeting about the May Day Fair?"

"Yes, I am thinking of making a few little things to sell, if I can get a table. Young Sofie is going to help me."

"I heard that Andy was getting some trestle tables, I should contact him and see if he still has one to spare. I think he will be as the meeting on Friday."

"I will do that," Tina said. "Will this rain never stop?" Meggie said as she passed Sofie in the street on her way in.

"Morning Sofie, Meggie said in passing.

"Hi Meggie, terrible day?"

"Can you believe his weather," Tina commented as Sofie walked in the front door of the shop holding an umbrella and a large shoulder bag. The umbrella did not seem to have stopped her from getting well and truly drenched.

"My goodness you are soaked right through," Tina said.

"Yes, it was so nice yesterday, I walked on the green and it was so peaceful." Sofie remembered the birds trilling from the branches, their tiny bodies, and fluttering wings. "The cherry blossom was so lovely. It really lifted my spirits."

"Are your spirits low Sofie?"

"No, well no not really, it's just that, I feel a bit worried about things."

"Why?" Tina asked.

"Something feels weird in the village, what is happening here?" she asked, "only yesterday it felt like spring ..."

"These are strange times," Tina mused.

"Yes, some things are not making a lot of sense at the moment, the weather the toads..."

"You have seen them as well?"

"Yes, outside the house yesterday and when I went to empty the bin, this morning there were dozens of them large and small."

"I had wondered if it was just me," Tina said, "it's very odd and no mistake."

"It surely is," Sofie said. "I feel very wary, like something bad is going to happen," Sofie said. "Do you know what I mean?"

"I think I do, Sofie," Tina said, then she smiled. "But I am sure we will be okay. Don't let it worry you."

"I won't Tina, and we have this May Fair to look forward to."

"I have some ideas about that," Tina said. "What would you say to us making some things to sell?"

"What a good idea," Sofie replied. "I have some ideas."

"We could make some cushions and herb bags. Will you help me?"

"I will, it will be fun," Sofie answered. "I think we could make some aprons and oven gloves, what do you think?" Sofie asked. "I could embroider them, and they would be so pretty."

"I can see you have really thought about this Sofie, "Tina said. "I think we will do very well together."

"Thank you, Tina, I enjoy working with you."

"I am glad to have you here Sophie. It is almost like…"

"Dear Tina do you still miss your daughter?"

"I do, and the worst thing is not knowing what happened."

"I can't imagine what it must have been like. Are you okay with this May Fair going on?"

"Yes, I think it is time to move on. And you are a big help Sofie, I mean that." Tina took Sophie's hand. "You are good company."

"Thank you. I love working with you."

"I love having you here," Tina said, "Let's get busy and make up some beautiful things to sell. I have half a roll of checked gingham that got left over from a job I did last year; we can use that."

"Yes, let's get started," Sonia said. "It's going to be great to have a May Fair again."

"It will, and I have to move on from the death of my daughter. With your help, we will make this May Fair a success."

"I feel certain it will be one to remember," Sofie said. "Are you sure you are aright about it?"

"I feel strongly that it will be great, I have to move on," Tina said but she turned away from Sofie, and picked up a roll of cloth. Her words were encouraging, but underneath she was feeling very apprehensive.

'I must put my daughter's death behind me now and start to live for the future. Anyway, what could go wrong.' Tina thought.

Tina pulled herself together and handed Sofie the bolt of cloth.

"Here this should be good for some items for the fair and we have lots of trimmings and ribbons that we can use."

"We are going to make it a day to remember, Tina," Sofie said as she took the roll of cloth. "And we are going to make some lovely items to sell. It's going to be great."

"It is doing be fun," Tina said, "I will look and look and see what other fabric we can use."

Tina watched as Sofie stated to roll out the cloth and take measurements. And she smiled at her enthusiasm. 'Maybe it will be alright after all,' he told herself.

Chapter fifteen

The village in late March 1959

"I'll get some proper posters printed and we can put them in the shop windows," Jim said as he bustled off to his office to design the poster. "And an advert in the local paper, that should spark some interest."

'Jim seems very enthused with the idea for a May Fair. Good that will keep him busy for a while," Brenda thought to herself, she yawned and stretched her back. "I can get through this, she said to Terry who had followed her in from the kitchen and then sat down at Brenda's feet as she started to read her book. "Thank goodness for the traveling library," she muttered then sniffed the air, "but first I have to take those biscuits out of the oven before they burn."

She felt a bit edgy; it was not easy living with someone you hated, well hated was maybe too strong, but she certainly had contempt for her husband.

"I will go potty. What a boring little place to be abandoned in." she told Terry. He wagged his tail and seemed to agree.

At that moment Brenda noticed that Anne Longland was approaching down the path and a moment later the doorbell rang.

Brenda was glad of the diversion. But did find Anne a bit dour, she was always moaning about her sister Jilly, the pair were like chalk and cheese. But Anne was one of the few people that attended Jim's church services.

Brenda opened the door and could tell straight away that she was in for some bemoaning about Jilly, because of the sour look on

Anne's face, and the heavily marked sense of resentment she radiated.

"Come in, come in, would you like a cup of tea and I have just made some biscuits, they are still warm?"

"Yes, that would be lovely," Anne replied taking off her coat and folding it up neatly and putting it on the side of a chair. She was dressed in a rather stuffy looking dress, that could be ten years old and the colour was the grey side of dull pink, with a little lightning like pattern in red. It looked clean and ironed, but very lose on Anne's' angular frame. Anne sat primly on the sofa, back straight, and knees together, looking very like the ex-school mistress, that she was.

Brenda thought that she must have been a formidable teacher, very stern and practical, but probably not a very popular.

"I am so glad you called," said Brenda, "if we are going to have this May Day Fair at the church hall, we have to plan it out, do you have any ideas?"

"It's a lovely notion," Anne said," but we will have to be careful that people realize it is a religious festival, a Christian festival, there is so much of this new age stuff going around now,"

"Well," Brenda started to say, "May Day is founded on old fertility rituals and Easter is based on a lot old pagan lore like the Easter eggs and hot cross buns…"

"Stop." Anne spluttered. "Just stop."

Brenda could see Anne turning a puce colour. "Are you, all right?" she asked, Anne looked about ready to implode.

Anne took a deep breath and looked down at her hands, calming herself before she spoke. "These are not God's ways."

"Anne, my dear," Benda said. "There is no harm in these old customs."

"I have had enough of this pagan drivel, what with Jilly making all those indecent figurines. I nearly died when I saw her latest creation, she is possessed by the devil, I swear, and then selling in the terrible new woman's shop in the village..." Anne was referring to Alana's gift shop. "She is a witch; I swear she is," Anne spluttered, "we should do something. She is a bad influence on Jilly."

Brenda sighed. "What can we do? She is not doing anyone any harm, and her goods, they are a bit controversial, but they are not illegal or anything." Brenda was starting to regret opening the door to this tiresome woman.

Anne had gone very pale and even seemed to be shacking, her hand repeatedly smacked against her own hip, and she looked off into the corner of the room hardly listening to Brenda.

"What do you think to some Apple bobbing, a fancy-dress competition and games for the children?

"What are you talking about?" Anne looked back at Brenda confusion.

"For the May Day Fair," Brenda replied, desperately trying to change the subject, and trying to think of a way to get rid of this boring, pious old woman. She was not in the mood; it was enough to have to cope with her husband at the moment.

"And a cake making competition? I tell you what," Brenda said,

"You come up with some ideas and present them at the meeting on Friday night in the village hall."

With this she stood and handed Anne her coat. "I will see you Friday then."

"But … I want to…" Anne started to say. "We need to make sure this is a religious meeting."

"We will, see you soon," Brenda said guiding Anne to the front door. "Goodbye."

Anne somehow found herself back out on the street, not having vented her feelings about her sister or the state of the village. She returned home with a face that could chew rubber tyres, an unfulfilled spinster, full of disappointment and unreleased anger that pent up in her until she thought she was going to burst.

"Why does nobody listen to me?" she exclaimed. "This village is headed for hades. I won't have it! Someone has to do something."

Chapter sixteen

March 1959

The second meeting in the Church Hall, was very well attended and it seemed that almost everybody had ideas for the May Fair. Father Jim welcomed everybody to the hall.

"It is wonderful to see the community come together," he said, "my wife and I are overcome with offers to help."

"Have we agreed on a day? As May the first is a Friday," Molly asked.

"I think that Saturday would be ideal for the May Fair, but we will be having a church service followed by a social evening in the hall on the Friday night."

"That is good," Anne said. "We must remember..." then she suddenly went silent and made no more comments, in fact she seemed to be in some sort of trance and left the hall a little later, on her own.

"Is she okay," Tina asked Jilly, who was sitting in front of her.

"I don't know, she has been acting very strangely, of late," Jilly replied, "or more strangely that usual."

"I have not seen much of her lately, not to speak to," Tina asked. "I take it you have not told her about our women's group?"

"Good God no, she would not understand." Jilly said.

"Quite right, how are you getting on with making things for the fair?"

I have made a few little figures, copies of some of my larger work and some decorative wall plaques. I thought that they might sell, and I can take orders for customized ones, with a house number or name, what do you think?"

"That sounds like a great idea," Tina said. "You have made me think…"

"And you?" Jilly interrupted.

"I have been using up scraps of material and making little herb bags and a few cushions," Tina replied, "Sofie has been helping me and she has some wonderful ideas for other products. And I have had some business cards made to hand out."

At that moment Father Jim spoke up. "Ladies and gentlemen, if I could have your attention, please."

Having reclaimed the attention of the gathering Jim related some of the ideas for the May Fair.

"People come forward from local villages asking to be included. A delegation from the local Women's Institute in Smalltown, have asked if they could run a cake and craft stall, and they volunteered to run a cake making competition."

"That good," Brenda said, she was delighted, at this because it was not a chore she would relish.

"We have had a brilliant response from our posters," Father Jim told them. "One lady phoned to offer face painting service for the children. And the local estate agent offered them the use of a bouncy castle, provided that they could put up some advertising. A plant nursery near Illminster wants to do a flower display and some tutorials on flower arranging, and they had their own marquee, which could be used for this purpose."

Father Jim paused, "What else was here dear," he asked Brenda, she looked down at her note pad.

"An ice cream man and a mobile burger bar asked if they could pull up on the day," Brenda said, "and a basket weaver from Moeston wants to demonstrate willow weaving and sell his wares, trugs and baskets and pot holders."

"What is a trug?" Tina asked.

"It's a shallow basket you would use picking flowers of collecting vegetable from the garden." Meggie said.

"Thank you, Meggie, for clearing that up for us," Jim said with a smile, inclining his head once more towards his wife.

"And I can make some flans and more healthy things to eat," Jilly said.

"I can help with that," Molly volunteered, turning to Jilly, who nodded.

"That great, Brenda replied, "I can do my bit there with some savory dishes and salads, let us get together ladies and make a plan," Brenda said indicating to Molly and Jilly, "See me after the meeting," They both nodded and the meeting resumed.

"All in all, things seem to be coming together very well," Jim said. "According to my list we seem to have plenty of volunteers."

Andy came in late as usual, but he had news.

"I have located a company that hires trestle tables. I can order as many as are wanted, very cheaply," he announced.

There was a scramble of people asking for more information.

"If you could see Andy after the meeting, please, then he will know roughly how many we need, okay Andy?" Jim said, then he turned to Brenda. "Can you liaise with Andy on this?"

"Yes, she said," Brenda looked over at Andy as he was already making a note of people who wanted a table, when he looked up at her and smiled.

Brenda flushed and turned away. Andy smiled to himself and continued making notes.

About an hour later the meeting stated to break up, a lot had been achieved, and Jill had a notebook full of suggestions, and queries.

"That went very well," Jim said to Brenda. "I had no idea what we were taking on. You look tired, my dear is everything okay?"

"Well, yes, it is a bit overwhelming. I will tidy up here and then I will take a long hot bath, I think an early night is on the cards."

"Quite right, my dear, you do that. I want to make some notes and then I will work on my sermon for Sunday. I think I may get a few more people this week." He smiled distractedly at Brenda and left her in the kitchen standing next to a pile of dirty cup and saucers.

Brenda sighed. "You do that," she said bitterly as she turned on the hot water, "I'll just clear up here, shall I?"

Brenda started to load the cups and saucers into the sink when she saw a movement in the kitchen, by the door. "What is that?" she asked herself. She walked over to the back door and saw a large spotted toad sitting there. "What are you doing here?" she asked, and opened the door to usher it out, but as she did so, several other toads hopped in and Brenda grabbed an old broom that was standing in the corner by the fridge and tried to repel them. But they just kept coming, until Brenda ran screaming to the house calling for her husband.

"Whatever is the matter?" he said running from his study.

"Toads, Toads," Brenda yelled, "hundreds of them."

"Where," her husband asked.

"In the kitchen of the hall and outside," Brenda was quaking with fear and flopped down in a chair in the kitchen.

Jim rushed out the door.

"I'll go see," he said. "Come with me Terry."

Brenda got up and stumbled over to the sink and looked out the window and then decided to put the kettle on.

"I could do with something stronger," she thought to herself. Then she could swear that she heard a cackle of laughter, and the window rattled in its frame, she looked up and saw a shadow, then it was gone.

"Now I really need a drink," she said to herself.

Terry had followed Jim, and she could hear him barking outside, in the hall, but then Jim returned with Terry at his heels.

"I don't see anything," he said. "You look really shaken; shall I get you something to drink? A drop of whisky perhaps?"

"But they were there," Brenda said putting her hand to her face, "dozens of them."

"Well, they are gone now, Terry must have scared them away," Jim replied, "are you making tea?"

Terry went over to Brenda and rubbed his cold nose on her hand, Brenda jumped, and startled the dog.

"Sorry Terry, I am a bit on edge, do you want your food now?"

Terry barked and looked up at her as if he was starving. "Okay boy, just give me a minute." Brenda said, she was still very shaken.

"I will call the Rentokil people in the morning, and ask them what we should do, that ought to sort it," Jim said, sitting down and looking at his note pad.

"You okay pet, you seem a bit jumpy," he asked, forgetting his offer of getting her a strong drink.

"Just tired I think, not been sleeping well. Brenda said, "I think I will have a cup of cocoa."

"Good idea, and then why don't you get an early night," Jim looked up at his wife. "I am sorry that things are so difficult," he said.

"Yes, Jim, I know you are, but it is not easy for me you know, and this May Fair is going to be a lot of work."

"It is, I agree, but it will let us get to know the community better, life will get better, for us, "Jim said. "Please believe that."

"I hope so," Brenda said, and then she turned away and went up the stairs to bed. "But I don't see how," she muttered to herself.

Chapter seventeen

The village April 1959

The door of the Pandoras box opened and Anne entered, she looked pale and manic and she was carrying a large bread knife. A moment later in rushed Jilly, who stopped still as if frozen when she saw that Anne was standing in front of Alana with the knife raised in her hand pointing at Alana's heart.

"Alana," she cried, "she is raving, please be careful."

A black void of Anne's thoughts pressed into Alana, leaving a path of queasiness and disgust. Anne was so thick with the ancient one, the witch Maud, that you could see her inside her black eyes. The raw hatred was terrifying. Alana felt her knees tremble and buckle, but she held firm, squeezing her fists to give herself the strength to remain standing.

"Be gone," Alana shouted. "This is not your time."

The howling thoughts of the witch echoed through the room. It was a deluge, just like when the rats on the rubbish dump ran into the streets, after the floods.

"You evil thing you, Anti-Christ," Maud shrieked, with Anne's voice. "I will have my revenge, you cannot stay me, this is not your business."

"Be gone," Alana shouted again. "Be gone, this is not your time."

Anne's eyes burned with rage and she took another step towards Alana. Jilly was shrinking down behind a display of greetings cards, holding up her hands as if afraid that she too would be murdered.

"Anne, stop," Jilly yelled, "stop for God's sake."

"I will have my vengeance," Anne shrieked and then she dropped the knife, and collapsed on to the floor.

"Is Anne still in there?" Jilly asked. She was looking stunned and not a little afraid. "She tried to kill you. I tried to stop her but... I think I might faint."

Alana pushed Jilly into a chair and went for a glass of water, and then reached behind the counter for a bottle of whisky and took a gulp, she then offered it to Jilly, who shook her head.

Jilly had heard Alana speak, but had not seen the spell that Alana had made to stun Anne, but she was too traumatized to notice much of anything.

"I think that she has gone for the moment, but ..." Alana said, "But maybe we better tie her up, and call an ambulance."

"What is going on?" Jilly said, she was acting strange and I saw her pick up the knife so I followed, my god she could have killed someone."

"Jilly, Jilly, I think she is possessed, has she been behaving differently of late?"

"Well, she is always a bit strange, but the past few weeks she has been ranting and railing about almost everything, and the weather..."

"The weather, yes it has been decidedly peculiar the past few days. The weather, yes, Anne is causing that?" Alana said, taking another gulp from the whisky bottle. "How could I have missed this."

Anne suddenly sat up on the floor. "What is happening? Then her posture changed, even her appearance changed, she looked younger slimmer her colouring was different, long golden curly hair, sea green eyes, she looked around at Jilly and Alana. She jumped agilely to her feet and threw out her arms wide.

"I am Maud Longland, daughter of Alice Park …. I have come to revenge my mother's death and I will not be stopped."

Then she fainted and fell unconscious to the floor, once more.

Jilly looked horrified." Maud Longland?" she murmured. "Did the Queen know about this?"

"I don't think so. This is powerful stuff, I think you sister is possessed by a witch, a very powerful and pissed off witch and your ancestor," Alana said and turned her face away, thoughtfully, so that Jilly could not see the wonder and excitement that crossed her face. "I am going to need some help with this."

"But … but how can that be, she is such a devout Christian, always goes on about the church and what is right and moral," Jilly looked down at her sister who seemed to be coming back to herself.

"Evil has a strange sense of humor, but it usually goes to those that have fanatical belief or weak intellect."

"What is happening," Anne said the she looked up at her sister, "Did I fall?" she asked. Now seeming to be back to normal.

"Yes Anne … you came over all queasy, let us get you home, and have a nice hot drink, then I think you should go to bed have a rest for a while." Jilly picked up the knife and deftly handed it to

Alana, who put under the counter and covered it with some wrapping paper.

With the aid of her sister Anne reluctantly rose from the floor and walked, somewhat unsteadily, out of the shop, Jilly looked back at Alana.

"Should I get a doctor?" she asked. "Alana my dear, she could have killed you, I could not have born it."

Alana shrugged her shoulders, she now had a lot on her mind, could it be Anne? Could Anne be the conduit from the witch, Maud, she has re-activated the curse? I best get on the Queen she will know what needs to be done. "I think there is more to this than we suppose."

Alana whispered, "This is no simple assignment, maybe not so boring after all."

As she picked up the phone, then she shivered with excitement.

Chapter eighteen

London, Sloane Square. Early April 1959.

On a corner of Sloane Square near Peter Jones, there was a large mansion house. The only thing was that if you did not know it was there and you could not see it, because it was hidden by an invisibility spell.

Only witchy folk and their invited guests could enter, most people just walked past on the way to the station and did not even know of its existence.

The Witch Queen Emelia Rey kept a luxurious house, nothing but the finest Chrystal chandeliers and silk furnishing were good enough for her. But when she could just change her décor in a flash, she never became bored, although she did still get very testy, if things did not happen as quick as she would like.

Emelia Rey has just emerged from her scented bubble bath and had put on a gorgeous flame colored robe. She approached her female attendant and she knew she smelled and looked magnificent. Emelia Ray was a very striking looking woman, with or without the glamour's that she frequently used, to pass in this modern world.

"Bring me silk cushions and Arabian carpets Hermosa," she ordered the girl. Her latest decorating theme was Arabian nights, mixed with art deco, it was an interesting mix.

Emelia entered her upstairs bed come sitting room and leant over to stoke Ebony, who peered up at her, with deep mesmerizing green eyes, that seemed to look into your soul.

"Are you okay my dark hearted beauty?" Emelia said, "are you hungry? do you want some nice fresh meat?

"He was fed earlier," Kigali said as he entered the room with a tray of coffee and pastries. "A fine young goat, he should be satiated." Jacopo hated the black panther and always kept well away from him.

"Is that right my darling?" Amelia said, lowering herself the floor to kiss Ebony, he rubbed his face against her forehead, purring loudly.

"You love me don't you," Emalia murmured, while rhythmically stroking Ebony's head and back. Then suddenly the cat had had enough and with a flick of his tail he stalked away to sit on the fine Arabian rug next to the window, where he basked in the incoming sunlight, thern curled up and went to sleep.

The Queen elegantly shook her gown out around her and looking around, as if remembering that she was doing something.

Then glaring at Kigali, she asked.

"What news from Alana, has she found out who is re-kindling that old curse, it could upset the human world too much, if it continues for much longer or there will be serious ramifications?" Emelia said, putting her hand out and caressing a beautiful pink and gold silk cushion that Hermosa was holding. "That is so lovely Hermosa, curtains too please. For the oriental dining hall."

Kigali hovered nearby," Majesty," he started to say.

"Yes," Emelia Rey said, looking very irritated, and glaring up at him, "Is there news?"

"Yes, most beautiful Queen, most beloved of our age," the man replied, he was dressed as an Arab slave boy, and did not like it one bit. "She phoned a moment ago while you were bathing."

"What of the witches' curse? Have she heard anything?" Emelia asked, she was getting irritated, and it was not a good idea to irritate Emelia Rey.

Her female assistant was a very beautiful young women with long golden curls, and a very flimsy gown of flickering colours, and Kigali was a deep plum black man and very elegant despite the hated costume. Hermosa stood waiting for the Queens next orders; she was still holding the silk cushion.

"Shall I begin the ceremony," she asked, timidly.

"What?" Emelia said.

"You have invited those herbalist witches and warlocks to design a garden for the next Chelsea Flower Show, they are here to show you their designs," the lovely girl said.

"No wait, is there news from Alana or not, I want to know what is happening." Emelia addresses Kigali, "wake up, what is the news?"

Alana rose effortlessly to her feet and brushed down her exquisite gown which was changing colour to a more vibrant red as she became irritated.

"Her last message said that she was getting close to discovering the source," Kigali said nervously, as he backed away from the queen and glanced furtively at the panther, "and that she would report back very soon."

"I see," The queen said and waved him away. "You are dismissed.

Hermosa, take the horticulturists into the blue reception room, I will be there is a jiffy."

Queen Emelia Rey drank her coffee and then ate a delicious apricot pastry before she did a quick glamour, so that she looked her most fabulous best. She needed these country warlocks and witches to come up with something sensational for Chelsea, she would win this year, or they would all know about it.

She glamoured a gown of living plants lilies and lotus that seem to be growing all around her and extenuating her curves. Her long blond silky hair was held high on a delicate trellis that allowed it to fall like a golden waterfall into the blue background of her gown. She floated out of her bed chamber and down into the Heavenly Pacific Island reception room, a fixed smile on her face.

"Come Hermosa and Kigali, we will go down together," the Queen ordered. "And you, Ebony, my dark angel."

The panther stretched and joined his mistress as she descended the stairway with her attendants. Everybody gasped when she entered the room with Ebony beside her and sat on her throne. She was followed by Hermosa and Kigali who were both stunning looking individuals and made quite a magnificent impact when seen together. Hermosa so pale and golden and Kigali so black and dignified.

"Right, what have you got to show me?" she asked as she suddenly materialized among them. "I am warning you. I am not in the mood for failure."

Chapter nineteen

The village 1600's

When she was still a young girl her stepfather gave her a nanny goat. Maud loved that goat, and it would follow her around like a pet. The goat had two tiny kids, that Maud helped deliver.

"My clever Matilda," Maud said, "my precious little friend." Maud was helping Matilda to clean and then feed her tiny kids. The animal loved her and was happy to share her offspring, with this fey beautiful child.

After loaning the services of a ram there were two more kids. Maud started to milk the goats and then started to make cheese, her little herd grew in size and before they knew it, Maud had a little business going.

"Can we get some chickens?" Maud asked her stepfather one day. "We could have fresh eggs every day, and maybe some to sell?"

"You know we have no land to keep them on, Maud," Johan Longland said. "We can't put up a chicken run on common land."

"It seems such a shame, she loves those animals and I think that they love her, and we could do with some extra income, Johan," Jean Longland replied taking his hand in hers, "do you ever regret taking in the child," she asked.

"Never, I love her like my own," he replied. "As do you."

Lady Elizabeth Frost still visited the girl regularly and was enchanted to see Maud's affinity to animals. She loved the child very much and wished that she legally was a part of her own family.

"She is at one with nature that girl," Lady Frost said one day when Jean and Elizabeth Frost were sitting watching Maud with her animals.

"Indeed, she is," Jean replied, "she has so many ideas, for chickens and selling the eggs, for making cheese, but as we have no land of our own, I don't see how she can continue. We can't enclose any of the common land, and to keep chickens we will need a chicken house and such, it is impossible."

Lady Frost sat back and watched the beautiful child, now nearly ten years old and her expression was provoking. "Maybe," she mussed.

"What that my lady?" Jean asked.

"Nothing my dear I was just thinking."

Lady Elizabeth Frost's health was not good, she was in a stressful relationship with her husband who always seemed to have more important matters to concern him than this wife. She did not get on well with her son Gerald, who rarely spoke to her, even when he was at home, he was out shooting things and getting drunk with his crony's, but he spent most of his time up in London with his wife.

"I never see you son," she said on one of his rare visits, "could not your wife and children come to stay now and again?"

"You know that Caroline does not like the country, but I will ask her," Gerald answered, "okay Mother, now I must go and meet the boys, we are going to ride over to the moor and do some shooting." he said as he swept out of the room. "There will be game for lunch tomorrow."

Just a few months later Lady Frost became ill, and in a matter of months she was dead. A few weeks after hearing of the Lady Frosts demise, a man came to the door of the Longland house asking to speak with Maud's guardians. He was very smart and carried a leather briefcase.

"How can I help you," said Johan, nervously.

"I am a solicitor, and I come here as executor of Lady Elizabeth Gloria Frost? "You are the legal guardian of one Maud Park?" he asked.

"Yes, my wife and I took her in, and pronounced that she be one of my family," he replied, "and she has taken my name as her own, Longland." "Her name is now Maud Park Longland?" The solicitor asked, making a note on his papers.

"Yes, we had it registered in the church records," Johan said.

"Maud Park Longland, once daughter of Alice Park?" the man repeated.

The man looked down at the papers in his hands and made a note before looking up again.

"And you, Mr Johan Longland, are her legal guardian?"

Johan nodded. "What is this all about? Is it something to do with our Maud?"

"Do you read? Mr Longland," he asked.

"A little," Johan replied, "so do my children."

"Well," he said ponderously, "Lady Frost had a little income of her own," he paused, "and she has left a small parcel of land plus one hundred pounds to your adopted daughter Maud."

"My goodness," Johan said, "can I call in my wife?"

"By all means," the solicitor said, smiling beingly.

"I will get some refreshments; would you like some ale?" Johan said as he left the room.

"That would be very nice," the Solicitor replied. "If is no trouble."

A moment later Jean Longland came into the room and shakily put down a tray with three mugs of ale and some handmade cake and biscuits.

"Good morning, sir?" she asked.

The solicitor had stood up as Mrs Longland entered, and Jean signaled for him to sit again.

"Would you like a piece of honey cake? "Jean asked shyly.

"Why, thankyou Mrs Longland, that would be most welcome."

Johan Longland followed her thirty seconds later, looking somewhat bemused.

"I was explaining to your husband that Lady Elizabeth Frost, has left your Maud a legacy," he said with a smile," she was by all accounts very fond of the girl."

"Lady Frost came to see her regularly before she fell ill. Maud really missed her," Jean said, she was feeling quite overcome by this news. "We sent some flowers. I don't know if they ever received them."

"The Frost family have tried to challenge this gift, but the will was made legally and registered with my office and cannot be contested." The solicitor seemed very emphatic on his point, "But there are some conditions, to the legacy."

"Oh, and what are they?" Joan asked.

"The will specifies that the land must be used for a small holding, on which there is to be a chicken run and goats and cheese making."

"But…" Johan started to say.

"There can be no buts, this was her condition. You and your wife are authorized to help start the little business, but when Maud comes of age, she will be the owner, is that understood?"

"Perfectly," Johan replied.

"Now, all I have to do is get you both to sign some papers, and I will need to meet Maud, she also needs to sign a document, is she around?"

"Yes, I will go get her," Jean said rising from her seat.

"First, I need your signature please, Mrs Longland."

When little Maud came in the room some minutes later, the solicitor was stunned, 'what a beautiful little girl,' he thought.

"Come my dear, has your mother explained what is happening?" he asked Maud.

"Yes Sir, my aunty, I mean Lady Frost, has left me some land to have my goats and chickens on, is that right, sir?"

"Yes, it is my child," the solicitor was quite taken back by the charm and worldliness of the pretty girl in front to of him, "she cared for you very much," he said.

"I loved her too," Maud replied.

"I believe you did fair Maud. I wish you well," the solicitor said, "and if you ever have need of help, do not hesitate to let me know."

"Thank you, Sir, I will do that." Maud replied, and thank you for your time, it has been nice to meet you."

"My dear young lady, it has been entirely my pleasure," the solicitor said.

But when the time came that Maud did need his help there was little that he could do against the poison and jealousy of the time.

Poor Maud's future for a time was secure but, alas, it would not last.

The animosity of the Frost House would be her ruin.

Chapter twenty

The village 16th and 17th century

Years later Maud had grown into a lovely young woman and she had married, Henry, the oldest son of the Longland family and they had a son, Little Teddy. She had done well for herself and had a little homestead with chickens and goats, that bought in a small income. She was envied by the women of the village, because she was beautiful and loved by a good man and cared for by the Longland family. But they had kept the truth from her about her mother and her parentage.

But she found out, and started to ask questions, questions that the Frost estate, did not want dug up. There was enough shame in the family, their reputation had been tarnished by the behavior of David and his madness. This had tainted the Frost Family name and they were no longer in the privileged position they had had in the reign of Henry the eighth. The passing of subsequent Kings and Queens had left the country in a very muddled state. But still the witchcraft trials went on as religious persecution continued. Local people started gossiping.

"She thinks she is so high and mighty, but she is just a Frost bastard, one local woman," said loudly, as Maud and her husband passed.

"What did you say," Maud asked, turning towards the grinning woman.

"You heard I think, not so grand now," she mocked, turning to her companion, and laughing.

Maud glared at the woman and hexed her fingers, the woman blanched and stumbled, and then beat a hasty retreat. This fueled the gossip of witchcraft against Maud and rumor spread, she found that no one would talk to her, and they mistrusted the family. Lord French's surviving son Gerald heard about this and saw a way to rid them of this bastard, this tiresome woman who was now asking all sorts of questions and bringing up old resentments.

"Jealously can stir up a lot of malice, and much of it was directed towards Maud," her husband said. "She had always been envied by the resident trollops in the village."

When Maud was arrested, there was no shortage of witnesses against her when she came to trial.

"She hexed me in the street I have witnesses," a local woman stated.

Nobody came forward to defend Maud, they were all too afraid.

Even the lawyer, now an old man and retired, who had come to administer the will of Lady Elizabeth Frost behalf, could not intervene for Maud against the still powerful Frost family.

After she was arrested, Maud was starved and tortured for days on end and not allowed any sleep, but made no confession. But they did not need a confession, the allegations from the Frost family and from her neighbours was enough, she was to be put to the fire, to burn alive.

When Maud was found guilty, she was held in Exeter garrison until the sentence was carried out.

As Maud burned, she cursed the family and said, "Your seed will continue in jeopardy and your menfolk will die badly like weeds in the grass. This is my gift to you, the House of Frost."

Gerald Frost was married and had three children. Gerald's oldest son died later that same year of measles and the other boy was ill but survived, he married and had several children but did not live to see many of them past their tenth birthdays. Because he too died, of some unknown complaint, believed to be self-induced by his addiction for strong alcohol and going riding out to shoot at all hours of the day and night. He fell from his horse, caught a chill, and died on the ground, before his body was found by a local farm worker.

"That family is under a black cloud, and Maud Park Longland is the cause of it," a local grandmother told her children. "Their line is cursed."

It was a warning to the local girls, "beware who you consort with, a sugary trap will capture you good, there is no getting away, once ensnared."

Chapter twenty-one

The village, April 1959

In the days after the second meeting about the May Fair, Brenda had been kept very busy, answering phone enquiries, and organizing a list of the itinerary of exhibitors and vendors.

"Have you spoken to Andy about the trestle tables?" Her husband asked.

"Not yet, "Brenda replied, in fact she had been putting off going to speak to Andy. She was aware that there was an attraction between them, and not sure if she would be able to resist him, if he tried something on. "I will go over this evening," Brenda said.

"That's good, I am going to see if I can organize something for the Friday night service." Jim said. "The church in Ilminster has a choir, and I thought it would be nice if they came to us for the service and gave a recital. I spoke to their priest, Father, Jack, and he seems to think it would be a good idea."

"That is great, I think that people would love it," Brenda said. "We could do some simple refreshment in the hall afterwards."

Brenda was on tender hooks most of the day, she kept thinking about Andy. In the afternoon she took Terry for a nice long walk and when she came back, she had a shower and washed her hair, and even put on a nice new silky blouse with her best linen trousers before going over to see him.

"I am a fool," she said, "I don't want him to seduce me, but I will be very disappointed if he does not try."

Watching out in the afternoon she saw Andy's van pull up about four thirty and prepared to go and see him.

Jim had come in and gone out again, saying that he was meeting someone in Ilminster to talk about some Morris Men for the May Fair. He said he would probably be back late.

At five-thirty Brenda knocked on Andy's front door. After a short delay, he opened the door in jeans and t-shirt, he was not wearing shoes and looked as if he had just come out of the shower.

"I am calling at a bad time, I could come back," Brenda muttered.

"No, come in, I was just freshening up after a busy day, dirty job fixing someone's guttering," Andy said, "that heavy rain the other day has done no end of damage."

"Your hair is still wet," she said. "I should go."

"Don't you dare," come in and sit down and I will be with you in a minute."

Andy had nice hair, it was a rich dark brown in colour and very curly, worn long, nearly to his shoulders, he had an earring in one ear, a gold stud, Brenda had never noticed that before.

Brenda made herself comfortable on an old sofa, that looked as if it had seen better days, she looked around the room, it was clean and tidy if a bit sparsely furnished. Andy reappeared a minute later; hair obviously towel dried and unruly.

"I was going to have a beer do you want one?" he asked.

"Yes please."

"Just a mo. then," he said disappearing again into the kitchen, returning with two cans of Heineken.

"So, what can I do for you?" he asked.

"I have come to see what is happening about the trestle tables."

"Right, I have a list somewhere of people that put their name down from Friday," he rummaged on the coffee table and produced a notebook. "Yes, eight people said they definitely wanted one table," he concluded.

"Eight?" and I have a few people on the phone enquiring about things, an environmental organization, a local hospice and a delegation asking if they can raise awareness for a cancer charity," Brenda looked up at Andy, "and we want some for refreshments, so we could estimate maybe as many as twenty tables, do they have a limited number or is it flexible?"

"No, we can have as many as we like, but they need a few days warning and will deliver on Saturday morning."

"That should be no problem," Brenda said.

"You have a list? Let me see if we have any overlap," Andy said moving over to sit next to Brenda on the sofa.

He sat very near and their thighs were touching, Brenda was very aware of his presence and the lovely smell of a tangy shower gel.

"There does not seem to be any duplication," he said, looking up and gazing into her eyes.

She shivered and looked away quickly and could actually feel herself getting a bit flustered.

"Are you okay?" he asked, "you seem a bit tense."

"I am fine," she said, "it's just that things are accelerating very fast and I don't feel able to cope, and my husband…"

"What about your husband," he asked.

"I don't want to bother you with that," Brenda said, she was desperately trying to hold back the tears, she took out a hanky and blew her nose. "Got a touch of hay fever I think."

"Yes, it is bad this time of year, best to avoid the tree pollen, although that wind and rain has settled a lot of it." Andy was still looking at Brenda, and thinking she is in a high state of agitation, and surprisingly he found that he really cared about what was upsetting her.

"I went to see the Altar Stone last week, it's a very creepy place, do you know more about its history?" Brenda said changing the subject.

"Well, there have always been rumors that very odd things have gone on there over the years, occult and magic kind of stuff. I don't believe in magic, myself." Andy seemed a bit edgy about this subject.

"Nor do I, a lot of superstition and trickery." Brenda looked back up at Andy and before she could stop, the tears rolled down her cheeks.

"Whatever is it?" he asked, putting an arm around her shoulders.

"My life is such a mess. I hate my husband and I am trapped in this horrid place," she said.

"I sensed that you were not happy, do you want to talk about it?"

"No, not really," she muttered. "It is a bit complicated. I am sorry

I did not mean..."

"I see," he replied, but then he lent forward and kissed Brenda, she resisted at first, but then she returned his kiss.

'This not right,' Brenda thought, but she could feel her resolve melting, and deep in her heart, she knew it was really what she wanted.

She put her arms around him, and she felt her body start to react. He drew back from her and once again gazed deep into her smoky green eyes as he reached out and started to undo the buttons on her blouse. Brenda did not move, she wanted to give herself to him. When he had undone the blouse, he slipped it off her arms and put it aside.

"You so are beautiful," he murmured, lowering his head to kiss her shoulders and collar bones, his hands reached behind her and undid her bra. They slid down on the couch until he was lying beside her, kissing, and teasing her nipples, it felt exquisite. Brenda's hands started to roam over his body, she could now feel his arousal pressing hard against her thigh.

"Can we move somewhere more comfortable," he asked.

She nodded shyly, and he pulled her to her feet and led her into the bedroom. He kneeled in front of her undoing her trousers and pulling them down, as she stepped out of them, he kissed her stomach and breasts, making her nipples feel hard and sensitive. Then he stood up and took off his own clothes, she tried not to watch, but could not stop herself. He had a slim lithe body with very little body hair, and she could see the definite lines where the sun had not tanned his skin.

"Sit down," he said, and then he knelt before her. "Take off your panties, please."

When they made love, it felt like a release for Brenda, she had not had sex in more than a year and only now did she realize how much she needed that human contact. It had never been that good with Jim, even in the beginning. When they both climaxed together it was an explosion of emotion and liberation. Brenda gasped and nearly cried again.

"Well," Andy stated, "now that was magic!"

Brenda laughed, and then they found themselves laughing together, and then cuddling down on the bed, Andy's arms around her, and her head resting on his shoulder.

"I know nothing about you," Brenda said.

"Not much to tell, really, I am thirty-five years old. I was in the army but did not do active service, because of a childhood ailment that left me with dodgy kidneys," Andy stopped. "Do you really want to hear all this," he asked.

"Yes," she said.

"When I came out of the army, I was a qualified carpenter, and I found work doing some decorating and odd jobs, I moved to the village and … well that is about it. "

"What about family?" she asked.

"Gone long ago. I was an only child and Mum and Dad are both dead."

"You own your little house?"

"Yes, I purchased Dove cottage about ten years ago," Andy paused. "What about you?" he asked.

"Well, that is a much longer and much more boring story, and it will have to wait for another day, because I have to go. Jim will be back and wondering where I am."

As she tried to rise from the bed, he pulled her back and kissed her so passionately that she was tempted to stay.

"No, Andy I really have to go."

Brenda recovered her clothes and dressed, as Andy watched her. "See you again he said," and suddenly he realized that he meant it, he wanted to see more of this lovely lady.

"That will be complicated," she answered.

"You know where I live," he said with a grin.

"Indeed, I do." she paused, "Andy, I don't do this sort of thing…"

"I know," he said. "I know."

Chapter twenty-two

When Jim Noakes was at seminary school, he picked up some strange habits, and one of them was a predilection for female attire.

"Did you know that the Spanish word, vestido, for dress is masculine because it comes from the word vestments?" he told his friend Jeremy.

"No, I didn't, you come out with some very strange things, from time to time." Jeremy said, "Do you think this colour suits me?"

"It would suit me better," Jim said, picking up the beautiful pink blouse and holding it against his scrawny chest.

Jim and Brenda had married, after a very short association, they met because Brenda's father was an official in the church and Jim was one of his protégées. There must have been some attraction between, them but Brenda had long since realized that for Jim the marriage was only a steppingstone towards respectability.

'God only knows what I ever saw in him,' Brenda asked herself almost daily. 'I am trapped, trapped in a loveless marriage, and now trapped in this boring village.'

When it was discovered that Jim was a transvestite, Brenda's father moved heaven and earth to keep him in the church, but the outcome was to be sent to Little Barnstead, a small parish far from the sex pots and temptations of a big city.

"How did they find out," Jeremy asked.

"I was careless, I used to go up to town and change in a hotel room before going out, but this one time I was spotted by a friend of my neighbour, who saw me enter the hotel as Jim and later saw me return to my room as Jaqueline."

"Crickey, that was unlucky," Jeremy said, as he applied his lipstick in the mirror, "I think this my colour don't you?"

"Definitely."

"How did Brenda react, did she hit the roof?"

"She was surprisingly good about it, I don't think she cared that much about me being trans, it was just the neighbors and friends knowing, that upset her," Jim said, "We didn't have much of a sex life, but it all but disappeared after my secret was discovered."

"I am lucky I suppose, I live alone and, I don't have many friends, so I just live two lives, one is Jeremy, hot sales executive at work, and my other world as Gloria."

"Can I try on that red dress?" Jim asked, "it is such a lovely colour. Where do you get your clothes? You have such a great selection; I am quite envious." Jim picked up a pale blue suit, with a white lace collar and held it up in front of himself. "I love this one, it's just beautiful."

"Mostly by mail order, one can buy anything these days if one knows where to look." Jeremy said, "But there is a dressmaker in Bristol that will knock up anything you want."

"Is there? Sometimes I wear Brenda's clothes, she is tall and slim, so they fit me fine, I just try not to let her catch me."

"Does she let you dress up at home?"

"Not often, but very occasionally," Jim said, posing in front of the mirror before turning to Jeremy. "She does not like me doing it and makes me feel bad."

"Bad can be good," Jeremy replied, "Try this one, I think it will suit you and bring out your eyes." He handed Jim an elegant dark green dress.

"Oh, that is so beautiful," Jim said. "Thank you. I don't like having to hide who I am, I would prefer to have more freedom to express myself."

"That is such a shame, some men are lucky enough to marry women who are into the dressing up, my friend Fred/Freida for example, his wife actually buys outfits for him and helps with the makeup and everything."

"That would be so wonderful," Jim said. "Acceptance."

"So where does Brenda think you are tonight?"

"I am looking into the possibility of some Morris dancers for our May Fair," Jim said.

Jeremy burst out laughing. "You're having me on. Are you going to have a May Queen? I would just love to be a May Queen. Can you imagine it a pretty dress and flowers in my hair, what bliss?"

"What a wonderful idea, but no, apparently there was some nasty business some years ago and the May Queen was found dead. It is all a bit of a mystery, so there has not been a May Queen ceremony in the village since that day."

"What a shame." Jeremy said, "oh you look great in that, I knew the green would suit you, try it with the hat and veil, oh what a goddess."

When Jim had moved to Little Barnstead, he promised not to keep in touch with anyone from the trans community, but he had stayed in contact with Jeremy, and went to visit him every few weeks.

"You are only one I can relax with," Jim said.

"Come over any time," Jeremy said. "I love to see you, it is just nice to unwind, just us girls."

"If only we could go out and be in the open."

"It is not impossible if you are careful," Jeremey said. "Very careful!"

"What do you have in mind?

"Well, I am thinking of having a little party in May, for my birthday. Would you like to come?"

"Oh, yes please. Can I order a dress?" Jim asked.

"I don't see why not, here is the address." Jeremy laughed, "Get something special. Some of my friends really go for it."

"I will. I can't wait. Oh Jeremy. To be myself for one night."

"Then you shall my friend ... you shall."

"I will do it, or die trying," Jim said. "How wonderful."

"You will be a sensation; we will knock um dead."

Chapter twenty-three

Plans for the May Fair were progressing nicely, three local villages had asked to be represented. Their help with the organization, was a god's send. Two other priests, their wives and families were offering to help organize different aspects of the day, one priest, Jack, was the vicar of two small villages, Illminster and Smalltown.

The Women's Institute of Smalltown were a real boon, as they wanted to run the cookery and flower arranging competitions, and Brenda was only too glad to let them take it on.

"Thank goodness for the WI they are so organized, I don't know where to begin with all this, how much food should we supply do we want soft drinks as well as teas and coffees. I think I may go mad," Brenda said to her husband, "and what will we do if it rains?"

"There is something called rainy day insurance, Father Jack told me about it, he said he would send me some details."

"That is a good idea," Brenda said, "it would be a disaster it rained."

"We will have to trust in the Lord for a fine sunny day," Jim replied.

"I have started an account book and some petty cash, it is in the large biscuit box on the dresser, keep any receipts and write all expenses down in the book, so we can keep a proper record. Okay."

"You are getting very organized, my dear," Jim said going and looking at the account book. "I will put in the receipt for the flyers and newspaper advert. I hope that the local newspapers will come and cover the Fair on the day. That would be good publicity."

"Have you thought about getting some celebrity to open the fair, that would catch the newspapers attention?"

"Good idea, do you have you anyone in mind?"

"No, but I will think on it, I suppose we could ask Lady Frost if we are desperate," Brenda suggested.

"Let us hope we don't get that desperate," Jim laughed.

"Too true, "Brenda said. "Maybe someone in the village knows someone famous. I can ask around."

"You do that dear, meanwhile let's try and get everything organized as much as we can, shall we?" Jim replied. "I really want this to go well it would establish us in the community.

"I agree, Jim. We have to become an important part of village life and then … and then maybe life here will be more barrable."

"Oh Brenda, is that how you feel?"

"Some days I feel as if I am servicing a sentence." Brenda paused. "But I am sure this event and getting to know the villages will help. It will get better Jim. I am sure of it."

"I am sorry Brenda. I know I brought this on us. But please let's try and make the best of it."

"I am trying." Brenda turned to face her husband. "I am trying, you do know that."

"Yes, Brenda. We are both trying to make things better."

Chapter twenty-four

Easter came, and the congregations for Jim's services were growing larger. Brenda had decorated the church for Easter Sunday with sprigs of apple blossom and there were vases of daffodils and Dutch hyacinths dotted around the place, making it look quite festive. After the service Brenda supplied tea and coffee for the congregation,

"How are plans going for the May Fair?" Molly asked Brenda.

"Well, to tell the truth, I am feeling a bit overwhelmed," Brenda replied. "It's all happening so quickly."

"You do look a bit peeked," Molly said. "Look I can take over supervision the food, if that will make things easier?"

"Would you? That would help so much, I can still make some flans and salads, let's get together again and plan what we need." Brenda looked a little less tense. "Thank you, Molly you're a life saver, and that's a fact."

"It is no problem, I have already spoken to Jilly and she and Anne are more than happy to contribute, although." Molly Paused. "Anne is behaving a little bit peculiarly at the moment."

"Is she? I was wondering if it was just me," Brenda whispered. "Do you think she is under a lot of strain, or is it something else?" Brenda paused. "Is she difficult to get on with?"

"Indeed, Jilly and her sister hardly even talk to each other," Molly replied. "Personally, I think Anne is losing her mind."

"This is terrible, has she a history of mental problems?"

"I think she has always been a bit fey, if you know what I mean? But this religious mania along with bouts of, well raving tirades against people. That is a new thing."

"I did not see her in the congregation today, she has never missed a service before, while I have been here anyway."

"She did come in and then she left early, sat right at the back and was dressed in a long grey coat with a hat and veil," Molly said. "I did not see her but my boy Brian did, he never pays much attention to the service, he said he saw her come in at the last minute and then leave before the end," Molly paused, "very odd, don't you think?"

"Yes, I do." Brenda said. "She came to see me a week or two ago, and she was ranting on about her sister Jilly and about Alana who runs the gift shop, it was very disturbing. I could not wait to get her out of the house."

"I don't think you're the only one who wants to keep out of her way," Molly said, "not by a long shot." Molly paused again, "and Alana is very nice we all get on with her."

"I have not really met her to speak to," Brenda said, sensing Molly's somewhat brittle defense of Alana. "I want to go into the shop and buy some candles, and to have a look around. I can get to know her then."

Outside the church Meggie's son, Peter, was waiting, he was standing next to Lady Jane's old Bentley waiting for his mother and grandmother, as he intended taking them out for a meal in the pub after the service.

"Well, this is a surprise," Harry said, I have not seen you in ages."

"Hallo, how is your mum?" Peter asked, "still running that dress shop?"

"Yes, are you waiting for your folks?" Harry enquired.

"Yes, I am taking them out for a pub lunch at the Plough over in Illminster. They have a nice carvery there today. Down for the Easter, are you?"

"Yes, Easter break, from university. Mum likes to go church, not my thing really" Harry shrugged, "but I thought I would come to meet her."

"I know what you mean. Are you coming to the cricket match tomorrow? Andy in organizing it," Peter asked.

"Yes, I will be there, and Alfie will be back tonight, so he can play, he has good bowling arm." Harry said. "That's excellent, that's Alfie Travas, I remember that he was good at sports."

Peter when quiet for a moment, "you played together at school…"

"Yes, we were good mates." Harry said. "He's doing well at university, should get a first, I believe, and you, how are things with you?"

"My work has really taken off. I have a huge contract for the new road structure for the South East coast. Could be worth millions." Peter boasted.

"That great, well done." Harry said, but his concentration seemed elsewhere.

"I remember the girl?" Peter said wistfully.

"What are you talking about?" Harry asked, "what girl?"

"Your sister?" Peter exclaimed, "Janice!"

"Oh, you mean the thing we did," Harry said. "You mean that prosperity ritual, but it didn't work, did it? I don't remember much…"

"It did work, but we need a booster, are you up for it?" Peter asked.

"But we…" Harry started to say, he suddenly started looking very agitated. "What did we do?"

At that moment Anne came out of the church and the two boys turned towards her.

"Look at the state of that," Peter said, turning toward Anne. "Is it Anne Longland?"

Then Anne saw them and raised her arm, pointing in their direction.

"What are you doing here," she demanded.

"Minding our own business, "Peter retorted.

"There is something not right, not right… "Anne stammered, "You should not be here, then she shouted, "Vermin, that is what you are vermin, you should be extinguished."

"What. Why you old bag, how dare you," Peter said.

Harry had gone very pale and was backing away from Anne, he looked panicked ready to run. But Peter just stood his ground and glared at Anne. Suddenly Harry bolted and ran off.

"Go away, leave me alone," he called, before disappearing down the road.

Peter looked after him in amazement, then looked back at Anne, his face defiant.

"You are a murderer," she said, then Anne just stopped and glared at him. "You are vermin." and then she turned and marched off down the road talking to herself as she disappeared around the corner.

"What the hell," Peter exclaimed. "What was that all about? What does she know?"

Chapter twenty-five

The cricket match, April 1959

The day started well, the sky was blue, and a few little white clouds scudded across its surface. It seemed a perfect day for a friendly cricket match between neighbouring villages. Many of the people from the home village had turned up to watch the game and were making themselves comfortable on the village green, putting down rugs, having picnics and chatting.

"They are here," little Brian shouted.

"Good, you go and get everything ready," Bert answered.

It was one-thirty when the team from Illminster arrived and disembarked from a very old school coach. Some other supporters arrived in cars and a few on bicycles. The ladies made themselves comfortable in deck chairs or on blankets and settled down to have a good gossip while watching their menfolk play.

"What a lovely day for it," Molly said as she sat herself down to watch. She was so proud that her husband and her son were acting as officials for the match. "Just look at them in their whites."

The teams were ready, and a coin was thrown to see which side would start. "Heads, Little Barnstead wins the toss. Start," the umpire shouted, and the bats man got ready to throw his first ball.

Little Brian was acting as scorer, and he sat, all important, in the Score Box. Bert Travis was acting as umpire. The first ball went wide and there was a cheer from the side lines as the wicket keeper called it out. The second ball was hit high and caught by a lad from Illminster, to a muted cheer from the Little Barnstead side and jubilation from the men from Illminster.

"Howzat," yelled one supporter.

Then a high ball hit. "No ball," yelled Mr Travis.

"You must be joking," Andy said. "I was behind the line."

"Get on with the game," Mr Travis said, "it is as I called it."

Andy shrugged his shoulders and glared at Bert, and they continued with the game.

His next ball hit the wicket and he was out.

"Not my day," Andy said, retreating the field of play go to stand next to Alana.

Peter Frost took Andy's place and the game continued. As the day progressed, some of the local ladies started to get the tea ready, the match was to stop at four sharp and then the sides would be reversed. Sofie was seated with Molly and Alfie when she saw Tina arrive with her son Harry.

"I'll just go over and say hallo to Tina and Harry," she said.

Her brother and sister looked pointedly at each other; it was no secret that Sofie had fallen for the handsome Harry.

"Don't tease her," Molly said as she got up and joined Meggie and Jilly who were standing talking and watching the game, as the water urn heated for teas.

"Do we have enough sandwiches," Molly asked, "there are more people here than I thought."

"We will have to cope," Jilly replied, "hopefully they won't be that hungry."

"I still have the sponge cake and scones to get out, we will manage," Meggie said, her sunny smile was reassuring.

"I think we will be okay," Jilly said. "Quite a lot of people seem to have brought their own picnics."

The tea and refreshment were set up in a tent gazebo sort of structure, that belonged to Lady Jane. There was a tea urn from the village hall. There were some beers in an old dustbin, half filled with ice, keeping them cool and some jugs of squash, for the children.

"I think we are all ready. What the ... what's that?" Molly suddenly said. "Something is…"

There was suddenly a loud buzzing coming from outside, and abruptly Molly heard her husband's voice. "Get down, get down on the floor, quickly now," Mr Travis shouted.

There was a moment of complete panic as a swarm of bees invaded the green. Ladies screamed and children fled and were then caught by adults and pitched to the ground, "Lie flat and do not move," Andy yelled. "Lie flat."

As fast as it arrived the swarm passed, and people started to rise and look around.

"What the hell was that?" one of the Illminster team said.

"Bees, where did they come from?" his friend replied.

As Peter recovered from the bee swarm, he rose to his feet to find himself standing next to Alfie, they looked at each other in shock.

"What happened here?" Alfie said.

Then they felt it, a jolt to their bodies, and they simultaneously looked up and saw Anne Longland glaring at them. "Rodents," she yelled, "filthy murdering rodents."

Alfie and Peter fell to their knees, screaming, unnoticed by the milling crowd of startled people. Anne turned away and laughed. In all the confusion she disappeared into the crowd, the only person who witnessed this altercation was Alana. But Alana had other matters on her mind, as she watched Father Jim his face a mask, running off in a panic towards the trees.

Many of the ladies were crying, and trying to see to their children, very few people had been stung, only a few that had run and agitated the swarm, otherwise it was shock and a state of unbelief that stunned most of the spectators.

"I suggest we stop for tea," Molly Travas shouted, "If anybody needs first aid, go to the church hall, and Brenda will be there with some salve and whatever is needed."

"Yes, come this way," Brenda called, "follow me. A handful of people followed her to the hall, where she unearthed a first aid box. Andy had also followed her.

"I can deal with this. Do you want to make some tea?" Taking the box from her shaking hands, "it will help with the shock," he said gently patting her arm.

Brenda had not seen Jim and did not know where he had disappeared to when the bees came. In fact, he had run away and was at this moment he was in the clearing near the Altar stone almost hyperventilating with fear.

One woman had been stung on her face near her eye and it looked very painful, otherwise there were remarkable few stings.

"It really hurts," she moaned, "and I don't know where my husband and baby are." The poor woman was nearly hysterical, with pain and worry.

Andy soothed the sting with some antihistamine gel and calmed the lady. A few minutes later her husband arrived carrying a small crying boy in his arms, the man looked very worried.

"Are you okay?" he asked, rushing to her side. He hugged his wife and tried to calm the screaming child. Brenda offered them a cup of tea, and they seemed get much calmer and the boy quietened in his mother's arms. The few others that had been treated for stings then drifted off back to the green to reunite with their families.

"What happened here?" the remaining man asked, now sitting with his wife and child, the woman still seemed to be in shock.

"I have no idea," Andy said as he tidied away the first aid box. "If she gets any swelling or other symptoms go to the hospital, is she allergic?"

"Not as far as I know." The man replied. "Well, now my wife has calmed down a bit, I think we will go home, thank you for your help."

"I was glad to give it," Andy said walking to the door with them. "You take care now."

Andy returned inside and he took one look at Brenda's face, and opened his arms to hold her.

"What a horrible day," she said. "Bees."

"Not one of the best," he agreed. "We seem to be having some very strange occurrences in the village at the moment."

"Yes, we do," Brenda said snuggling into his shoulder. "I hate this place."

"Yes, rats, bees not to mention the odd weather."

"Yes, something very odd seems to be happening in this village."

"Then, why don't we leave?" Jim said.

"We can't do that, Jim."

"Why not Brenda, I want to be with you. We could start up somewhere new. …"

"Oh Jim, don't be so daft."

"I mean it Brenda. I have fallen for you."

"I think we had better get back and see how everybody is. Don't you?"

"If you say so Brenda, but remember what I said."

"I will … I will Jim."

Chapter twenty-six

When the bees started to swarm Jim just took off away from the cricket game, out of control he fled towards the trees. After he stopped running, his heart was beating so fast that he thought that it would burst in his chest. He lent forward, hands on his knees until he could calm the fluttering.

"What the hell is happening?" he said to himself. Then he looked around and found himself next to the little stand of trees at the far side of the green.

"Come to me," he heard a voice calling, "come to me now."

Jim continued until he found himself standing by the Altar stone, then he realized that he was not alone. Sitting on the edge of the Altar Stone was a beautiful young woman.

"I have been waiting for you," she said seductively.

Jim's heart felt as if it would burst, he had never in his life seen anything quite so lovely. She had long chestnut hair and deep set large brown eyes, her mouth a moist red cushion, arranged in a perfect half smile.

"You are so beautiful," he said.

She laughed, and it felt like heavenly music to his ears.

"I have come to set you free," she said, "to be what you want to be."

Her dress seemed iridescent, like a silky cobweb floating around her perfect body, and he wanted it, he wanted that dress for his own. Jim found it hard to catch his breath, as these feeling ran through his body, lust, envy, and euphoria.

"Come to me now," she murmured standing and opening her arms for Jim to come to her. "I will make you whole again."

"I am lost," he thought. "Or am I found?"

When Jim returned to the house several hours later, he found Brenda and Andy sitting at the kitchen table drinking coffee. Jim walked in the door, looking dazed and disheveled.

"What happened to you," Brenda asked.

"I got lost," he replied. "I am going to bed."

Brenda and Andy looked at each other in confusion as Jim disappeared up the stairs.

"What was that all about," Andy asked.

"I have no idea," Brenda answered, she shrugged her shoulders. "He gets a bit strange sometimes."

"I don't understand what keeps you together?" Andy asked.

"Nor do I, "Brenda answered. "Nor do I!"

Chapter twenty-seven

The village in the early 1700s

Before she died Maud had grown from a sensitive introverted young girl into a beautiful and confident young woman. She had been much loved in the Longland family and wooed by their oldest son Henry, who she married when she was just eighteen. A year after they were married Maud bore a child, little Teddy.

Henry with, the help of his mother, raised Teddy. The family continued to thrive despite the scandal of Maud's death, Henry managed to keep going, for his child, after Maud was burned as a witch, her life so tragically cut short.

Teddy had inherited not only Maud's land and business he had also inherited her talents and her way with nature and in particular herbs and natural remedies. As he grew older, he became well known in the area by those that wanted help, be it medicinal or other. At the age of thirty he married Demelza who was from a gypsy family.

Her people had come to the village in April, 1618. There was a spring market and they wanted to sell their wares. Teddy had met Demelza, as she was buying some eggs from his stall and he was immediately smitten.

"Beautiful girl," he said, "will you be mine?"

"Never will I belong to anyone, but I may stay with you for a while," she replied, with a toss of her black curly hair and cheeky grin. They married that spring in the gypsy way of jumping the broomsticks, and had a tumultuous relationship, she was a wild dark beauty, there was plenty of spice in their marriage.

Demelza gave him a daughter, Nanette, in December 1619, and then the following spring she was gone. When the gypsies returned again to trade in the village, Demelza left with them.

Nanette loved the wild Devon countryside she had a pony to ride, a henhouse busy with chickens, and a flock of goats who crowded around her whenever she appeared, eager to be scratched under their chins.

"How are you today," she would ask, "my fine beauties.

When she was very small, a tiny kitten was found in the barn and it adopted Nanette and followed her around.

"And where did you spring from, my little ragamuffin," she said, when he first appeared. She called him Imp, because he was a scrawny dusky little fellow and could be there one minute and gone the next. She fed him and kept him warm and he grew into a scraggy dark grey tom cat with the most inscrutable, deep green eyes, and he would tolerate nobody to touch him but Nanette.

"You're a wild one, aren't you Imp, where have you been?"

Then the cat could rub against the legs and purr when she stroked his fur.

"Yes, you love me now. But I bet you will be off again carousing with the local pussies."

Nanette understood that animals had their own reason for doing the things they did, she did too. She had inherited an independence and willfulness from her mother's people combined with her grandmother's affinity to nature.

"You are a spoilt brat," her grandmother would say, "I don't know why Teddy indulges you so. Can't you help out sometimes?"

She did help, as long as it was something she wanted to do, she would look after the chickens and the goats, she even made cheese and collected the eggs and sold them in the market. But she would do no housework, in fact she was rarely in the house, other than to eat and sleep and not always then.

"You are too like your mother, and you have her looks," grandmother said.

Nanette was slim and curvy, much admired for her dark curly hair and her bright hazel eyes, but no suitors came forward because she scared them with her wild ways.

"Who will marry you?" her grandmother asked.

"I do not intend to marry," Nanette said scathingly. "Why should I stand for some man telling me what to do."

"Don't you want a husband and a family?" her grandmother said.

"If I want a child, I will have one, but not yet."

"You are a disgrace child," Grandma Longland scolded. But it made no impression on Nanette, she just did what she wanted to do and that was the end to it.

Teddy had been nearly thirty when he married Demelza, he had worked hard his entire life and he was a strong man in many respects but when it came to his child, he just crumbled and let her get away with anything. Nanette knew this but she did not take advantage, because she loved her father very much.

"Are you lonely," she asked him one day.

"No child, I have you," Teddy said.

He loved her, and she was his world. Teddy at the age of forty-five, let Nanette run rings around him. She was a clever girl and she also had the ability to heal and work with herbs, as well as run the homestead, her talent was animals, they seem to respond to her, and do her bidding.

They made a good team, with his good works and healing and with the profits from eggs, goats, and cheese they made a decent living. But, the constant thorn in their side was the Frost estate, who never stopped trying to hassle the Longland family, because of the inheritance to Maud, that they still contested and lost, all these years later.

They latest bugbear affected the entire village, a brook that ran through the Frost estate and then through the village, was being dammed and polluted, because the heir to the Frost estate, Gerald's son, William, used it for a mill and distillery.

"He cannot do that," Grandma Longland said, "We have always had the right to the clean water from the brook and it is now it is putrid with their foul brew, cannot something be done?"

"What can we do?" Teddy replied.

"Confront him," Nanette retorted, "he is not a god."

"He thinks he is," her father replied, "but I will go and see Lord Frost," Teddy said, and that he did with a few other traders from the village.

Lord Frost was not inclined to listen, in fact he laughed at them.

"We will take you to court," John the butcher said, "I need that water to wash, prepare and my process my meat."

"Yes, we will not just stand by and see our living taken away," Teddy said. "We will take it to the authorities."

"You do that, and good luck to you," Lord William Frost sneered, "Your family has been long been a thorn in my side ever since that witch ruined my family name."

"They did that all by themselves," Teddy answered back.

"Get out of my house," Lord Frost shouted, "and do your worst.

They returned to their homes disheartened and angry. "I will go to see the magistrate," Teddy said.

Teddy Longland and John, the butcher did go to see the magistrate and he told them that their case would not be heard that the Frost estate had a right to use the water as they saw fit.

"You do not have a chance," the magistrate said. "The Frost family is still powerful in the area; your case will be dismissed."

Nanette was incensed when her father returned and said that nothing could be done.

"We will see about that," she said.

Nanette was used to riding wherever she liked and would often cross into the Frost estate. The following day when she was out, her path coincided with the younger son of the Frost household Piers Frost.

"Good day to you," he called out pleasantly as he passed her by.

"It is not a good day," she retorted.

He stopped short somewhat taken back by the sharpness of her tone.

"This is private land," he said defensively.

"Is it?" she said, "and the water is private as well, is it?"

Piers was not the heir, so he was not privy to the affairs of the estate he just bumbled along and let his brother deal with those matters.

"What's that you say," he asked in his confusion. All he saw was a very angry but decidedly pretty young woman.

"You tell your brother that this matter is not over," she said as she went to ride off. "We have a right to clean water."

"What matter, what water?" he asked.

"Your brother is polluting the water in the brook, and it is unusable when if flows through the village," she spat at him.

"I did not know," he spluttered.

When Piers returned to the house, he confronted his brother. "What is this about the water in the village William?" he asked.

When William explained, Piers was shocked. "But they need the water too, can nothing be done?"

"Why should we be concerned about the village, we have the right to use the brook as it crosses out land," William declared.

"But…" Piers started.

"Keep out of it and go back to your dalliances in London. Leave the running of this place to those who know what they are doing."

But the next day Nanette was riding, and it was William that she met.

"You are on private land wench," he said abruptly.

"I see no signs to say I cannot ride here," she retorted.

"Why you impudent girl, do not speak to me thus."

William Frost lashed out at Nanette with his whip and caught her across the shoulder. "That will teach you to backtalk to me, you ignorant bitch."

Nanette was furious and she turned to him in furry, "You will be unseated from your high horse, William Frost, mark my words."

William laughed and rode on his way, leaving a furious Nanette glaring after him, holding her bruised shoulder. But before he reached home a fox ran out of the bush and startled him, the horse reared and William Frost fell, breaking his back. He was not found until much later that day, as he lay dead on the ground.

Piers was shocked and bemused when he suddenly became lord of the Frost estate, but the first thing he did was to talk to the villagers and together they made a channel to divide the brook so that fresh water still ran into the village.

When next Nanette passed Lord Piers out riding, he gave her a shy smile and kept his distance. "That woman is dangerous," he said to himself, "beautiful but dangerous."

Chapter twenty-eight

When Jim abruptly took himself off to bed after the cricket match fiasco, Andy and Brenda sat and talked long into the evening.

"Is he okay?" Andy asked, "he seemed a bit out of it."

"Who knows," Brenda replied. "What a day," I don't know what is happening in this village, but something is very wrong here."

"I have to agree, the weather, bees, rats, it is very odd."

"Rats?" Brenda said.

"Yes, I was doing some work for Lady Jane last week, just some shelves and a new door for the outside workshop, when I saw a rat. There seemed to be a nest of them, because after the first one I saw about six others." Andy gave a shudder. "I cannot abide the creatures; they give me the creeps.

"That's dreadful," Brenda replied.

"Yes, I informed Meggie and she said the that she would call in Rentokil, to put down some traps."

"Did I tell you about the toads?"

"No, what about toads?" Andy said.

"Well, after the last meeting, on Friday, I was clearing up and I saw all these toads in the kitchen of the small hall. I called Jim to go out, but he did not see anything." Brenda paused. "I also heard this voice and saw a figure pass by my kitchen window, and what sounded like eerie laughter."

"Crickey, Brenda ..."

"I know you think it's crazy, but I swear that I saw them," Brenda said, "and I know what I heard."

"I believe you. Some odd things have been happening of late."

"Jim did not believe me, and Terry did not seem to notice anything unusual, and he is usually very sensitive to things," Brenda said. "Like when I went to the Altar Stone."

Terry raised his head, as if he realized that they were talking about him, and barked a couple of times, before resting his head again in his basket. But his eyed never left them. His soulful gaze seemed to follow Brenda as she moved about.

"He is a great little fellow," Andy said and then he stood up and went to stroke Terry. The dog immediately stood and leaned against Andy's legs, obviously enjoying the attention.

"He likes you," Brenda said as she sat down again at the table, "and so, do I."

"I have something to confess," Andy said, a twinkle in his eye.

"What is that?"

"Last week when you were out with Terry, I gave him a bit of fried bacon," Andy admitted.

"Why did you do that?" Brenda asked.

"So that he would like me, and I could get closer to you." Andy looked shamefaced but not contrite.

"You rogue," Brenda said but she could not help but laugh.

Andy walked over to Brenda and knelt on the floor in front of her and took her in his arms. Brenda responded to his embrace and pulled his head against her chest.

"You're not happy with Jim, are you?" Andy asked looking up into her eyes. "Why do you stay?"

"I made a deal with my father to stay with Jim. But you are right, sometimes I cannot abide him."

"Why did you make a deal? I don't understand."

"It is complicated," Brenda said.

Andy let his head rest against Brenda's breasts. "It feels so right to be with you, Brenda, can we ..."

"Not here, and not now. I will come and see you tomorrow, is that okay?"

"Anything you do is okay by me, as long as it is with me," Andy mumbled into her chest. "I am starting to really care about you Brenda. What happened to make things so difficult with Jim?"

"I cannot answer that just now, I will tell you another time."

Then Brenda stood up and pulled Andy to his feet and kissed him, her hands ran up and down his back.

"Brenda," he murmured, "please. If we are not going to go any further, I better go, or I may tumble you here and now on the kitchen table."

Brenda laughed and at the same time Terry barked. "What is it boy," Brenda said. "Do you need to go outside."

Terry barked again and headed for the back door, looking up at them with a woeful expression on his face.

"It is just like he talks to you," Andy said.

"Oh, he does," Brenda replied. "Jim does not get it at all, he is not really a dog person."

"Nor am I usually, but I like this mutt," he said giving Terry's ears a quick rub.

This prompted a nudge from Terry against his legs and another bark as Terry edged towards the back door.

"I think things are getting serious," Andy said. "I will walk out with you. It is getting pretty late. I best be off to my lonely bed."

"Poor you," Brenda said with a grin.

It was quite cool outside, and Brenda shivered as she stood into the front garden.

"You are cold?" Andy said, taking her into his arms. "You may still be in shock from the cricket match."

"I am okay," Brenda said, but she did not push him away.

Terry finished his business and returned into the warm kitchen leaving Andy and Brenda alone in the dark.

"Go inside and have a hot drink before you go to bed, maybe that will calm you," Andy said. "I don't know if that will calm me, I want to be with you." Feeling Brenda pull away he said, "Okay, I will see you tomorrow?" He looked up at the night sky, which was emblazoned with stars. "It's a beautiful night."

" Yes, it is," Brenda said, looking out over the common, where the moon was just rising over the trees on the horizon. "Tomorrow" she said, as she returned inside. "I will see you tomorrow."

"You had better," Andy whispered to himself. "I am falling love with you."

Andy walked over the road to the cottage, but before going in he stood and looked over the common. He could see the cluster of trees, that concealed the alter Stone, highlighted against the midnight blue sky. The Easter full moon was in the sky and seemed battling with some very bright stars for position.

For one moment Andy thought that he saw a flash of light over on the common near the trees.

'What's that'" he said to himself.

There was another flash of light, that could have come from a torch. But then it was gone.

'Probably just some kids up to mischief.'

Andy stood a few minutes, but he did not see any further lights, so he turned and entered his house.

'How on earth am I going to get any sleep?' he asked himself.

'Brenda, I am in love with you.' Andy thought. "This does not happen to me. What is going on in that marriage.'

Andy lay in his bed for a long time before finally sleep caught up with him, and his last thoughts were about Brenda.

"I want her for mine own," he whispered.

Chapter twenty-nine

On Easter Monday most of the villagers are still in a state of shock, how could things go so wrong?

"What a day, the match ruined, and the children scared out of their minds," Molly said. "Why did it happen?"

"I can only imagine…" Bert said, as he had early morning cup of tea with Molly.

"But what could have caused the bees to swarm like that?" Molly asked.

"It is possible that a new queen took flight and that the bees swarmed after her, to find a new nest site."

"Does that sort of thing happen often?" Molly asked.

"I really don't know a lot about it," Bert replied. "What is this about our Sofie and Tina's son?"

"She has a bit of a crush on him," Anne replied.

"He seems like a nice boy," Bert said. "Not that I know him well, but Tina is always pleasant."

"Yes, she is. Now I have to pop down to the shop for some bread," Molly said. "Will you get the kids up and moving? When I get back, I will make us all breakfast."

"I will do that, my heart," Bert said as he reached out and pinched Molly's bottom.

"Stop that, you silly old sod," she said. "I won't be long."

When Molly reached the village shop, that had a bakery, there were several other villagers waiting to buy fresh bread.

"Morning Molly," Tina said. "There is a lot of talk in the village about the ruined cricket match. Bees, for god's sake what is going on?"

"Bert said that it might have been a new queen and the bees swarming was because they were following her," Molly said. "Most odd, I have never seen anything like it."

"Thank goodness that there was nobody hurt too bad, quick thinking on your Bert and Andy's part, they took control, while we all panicked," Tina said. "Brenda really stepped in to help anyone that had been stung."

"Too true, it could have been much worse," Molly said. "It is so nice to have our boys back."

"It is," Tina murmured abstractedly. "It is very good to have Harry home."

"I hear that Harry is doing well at university." Molly said. "My boys are going out helping Bert today, some boundary wall to mend, or something."

"Yes, Peter is back at Frost house as well, we saw him drive in the other day in a very smart sporty looking car, he must be doing all right for himself," Tina said. "They were all at the cricket match yesterday of course."

"I had better get back with this bread or I will have nothing to give them for breakfast," Molly started to say.

At that moment the sales lady, Gladys, ran from behind the counter and screamed.

"What the hell?" and a large rat appeared and headed toward the front of the shop.

"Oh my god," Tina said, as several more rats followed and ran through the shop. Ladies were screaming and in the general mayhem a shelf was knocked, and several packets of cereal slid to the floor.

"Watch out," Molly shouted.

At that moment Molly was sure she could hear a cackling laugh come from outside the shop, but when she glanced outside the window there was nobody there or was there a shadow that seemed to flicker and was gone. Molly shivered. "What is going on here?" she asked herself.

The manager of the shop came running out from the back storeroom and tried to repel the rats, by making sweeping movements, with an old broom, to hasten them out the door. "Stand aside ladies," he yelled.

The rats seemed to take little notice of him, so he ran into the back of the shop again and he called the fire station. When the fire engine arrived, ten minutes later, the fire men were not pleased to be called out, because by the time that they got to the shop there was not a rodent to be seen.

"Try phoning the council office in the morning, they will look into it, it is probably a backup at the sewage pipes because of the heavy rain. Something similar happened a while ago," the fireman said, as he left the shop.

Then they were gone, and several quacking ladies, took a breath.

"What is going on in this town," Tina asked.

"Yes, what the hell is happening? Things are getting out of control," Glady's said. "This is not the first time I have seen rats and there have been the toads and bees, not to mention the peculiar weather."

"We have to do something," Tina said, "Before someone is hurt."

"We have to have a meeting," Molly said. "You let Alana and Jilly know and I will contract Mr and Mrs Potts the rest of the ladies.

"Tomorrow night, at the usual place?" Tina asked.

"Yes. Things do seem to be escalating," Molly said, "We can't let it go too far."

"Maybe the queen will send more help?" Tina said.

"I will have a talk with Alana and to Jilly," Molly said. "But now I must get some bread and go home and feed my family."

Yes, me too." Tina runed away to go home but her face was white with worry.

Chapter thirty

The preparations for the May Fair were progressing well, although a few things seemed to be going wrong, but with the help of Andy, Brenda always found alternatives.

Like when the people who were going to supply the soft drinks for the Fair went out of business suddenly. But with Andy's help she found another supplier. Brenda was relying on Andy, a lot, Jim went out quite a bit on 'May Fair' business as he called it.

But one day Brenda found makeup on his shirt. Lipstick and what looked like face powder. He had come home late the night before and Brenda did not have the will to confront him until the next day.

"Where did you go Monday night?" she asked, as she made breakfast the following day.

Jim seemed flustered. "Oh, I met with this man who wants to do a demonstration at the May Fair," he said quickly.

"What kind of demonstration?" she asked.

"Wood carving," he said quickly, "friend of mine from way back."

"What shade of lipstick does he wear?" Brenda said, turning towards him holding his discarded shirt and showing him the stain.

"I can explain," Jim said. "He … we it is not what you think."

"I expect it is exactly what I think. I know you are still seeing your transvestite friends," Brenda retorted. "I don't care, but please be careful, we will lose our livelihood here if you are caught again."

"I am sorry Brenda, I did try, but the compulsion is too strong." Jim stood head hanging down, as Brenda regarded him with pity.

"I know," she said, "I don't really care, but you must be more careful."

"Thank you, Brenda, I know you're not happy here, things will get better."

"Now where have I heard that before," she muttered. "Jim."

"What?" he said nervously.

"Is it not a sin to lie? Even about your obsessions."

Jim's face blanched, and he burst into tears. "I have tried to stop," he said

"I know, Jim, let us forget it," Brenda said. "Pull yourself together now."

Brenda turned back to her cooking, "Do you want bacon with your eggs?" she asked.

That afternoon she went over to Andy and they made love, but now Brenda felt no guilt. If her husband could have his illicit pleasures, then so could she.

Chapter thirty-one

Jilly called in the doctor to see Anne after her maniacal attack on Alana in Pandora's Box.

"I think she is suffering from stress, has there been any emotional problems lately?" he asked.

"No, Doctor Wilde, not really, we have all been working towards this May Fair, but I can't think of anything else." Jilly paused "But she does act strangely at times. Like she is speaking to someone that isn't there."

"Does this happen often? Or has it increased lately?" he asked.

"Yes, now I think about it she has been a bit worse lately."

"Well, I have prescribed some antidepressants, and a sleeping draft," she should take it easy, get a few good night's sleep, and I think she should be fine."

"Thank you, doctor, I will see that she takes them."

"Good, let me know if there are any further developments," he said, then he gathered up his bag and was gone.

Jilly put Anne to bed and gave her a hot drink, while she went off to the chemists in Moeston to get the prescription filled. When Jilly returned Anne was fast asleep, so she phoned Molly.

"Can you keep an eye on Anne for me?"

"I will check on her if you're not around."

"I am worried, she has been behaving so very oddly lately. I have a lot to tell you."

"A lot of odd things seem to be happening of late," Molly said. "Did you hear about the rats at the corner shop?"

"Yes, I did. And we have plagues of toads and the weather!"

"It is all a bit strange," Mollie said.

"Anne tried to attack Alana. I had to call out the doctor, she is under sedation."

"What … what happened?"

"I think she is losing her mind Molly. She is acting so strangely."

"I see try not to worry about Anne, I will see you at the meeting."

"Yes, see you at the Potts. I will explain things to you then," Jilly said.

"You must be very concerned?" Molly said.

"I am. You will be there for the meeting tomorrow evening?" Jilly said. "I may need your support."

"Yes, I will. Don't worry Jilly, we will get through this together."

When Jilly put down the phone, she said, "What is happening here? Witches, in my family? Bloody hell, what next?"

Chapter Thirty-two

Molly was not the first to arrive at Mr at Mrs Potts house for the meeting of the friends of Little Barnstead. Jilly and Alana and a couple of others were already there.

"Come in," said Sheila Potts. "Would you like a drink?"

"Why thank you, I would," Molly said. "Bert can't come, he is staying with the kids."

Molly went over to Jilly. "Are you okay?" she asked.

"I am a bit shaky, to tell the truth." Jilly replied.

"I am not surprised, it is quite a story, to be sure," Molly said. Before she could make herself comfortable the doorbell rang again. This time it was Tina and her friend Gladys from the village shop.

"Anne not coming?" Gladys asked.

"We don't think it wise at the moment," Jilly replied.

Jilly looked over at Alana. Molly patted Jilly's hand.

"I am with you, don't fret," Molly said.

Mr Potts handed around drinks and then nodded to Alana to start the meeting.

"Welcome one and all," he said. "I will turn things over to you Alana."

"Thank you all for coming at such short notice." Alana paused. "I am sure that you are all aware that some very odd things have been happening in the village."

"Yes, rats, toads, bees," Gladys said.

"Not to mention the contrary weather, "Tina added.

"Quite!" Alana interrupted. "I think you all should have the right to know what is going on." Alana looked over at Jilly, who nodded.

"I will Tell them," Jilly said. "Many of you know that I contacted the coven in Moeston, earlier in the year regarding some odd events that were happening in the village."

"Yes, and they contacted the Queen of the witches," Gladys said.

"But what is happening?" Tina asked. "Things have been acceleration of late."

"I am the representative of the Queen and I have been keeping her informed about the most recent events, Alana said. "The Queen, Emelia Rey, is most interested in getting to the bottom of what is happening here," Alana once again paused and looked directly at Jilly. "Are you sure about this Jilly?" she asked, Jilly nodded.

"Go ahead," Jilly said.

"We have all been aware of some odd vibes in the village for the past month or so, we now believe that a witch from the 17th century is trying to re-activate an old curse."

"What?" said Gladys. "An old dead witch. For heaven's sake."

"Some of you will be aware of the history of this village, in the sixteenth and seventeen centuries there were many witch trials in this area, at least three witches were captured, prosecuted and executed from this village." Alana stopped and looked around.

"One of these women was Maud Park Longland."

Nearly everybody turned and starred at Jilly.

"Yes," she said. "She was my ancestor."

"Well, I'll be," said Gladys.

"Is this true? Did you know about her?" Tina asked.

"I did not know, until Alana told me and then I looked it up in the parish records." Jilly said. "Three of the women that were executed were my relatives from hundreds of years ago."

There was babble of conversation for a couple of minutes, but Mr Potts banged on the table to get every body's attention back.

"I think there is more, you will want to hear," he said.

"Thank you, David," Alana said. "It would seem that this old witch is trying to re-establish a curse."

"But," Gladys said, then she turned to Jilly. "Anne? Oh my god. Is it Anne?"

"Yes, you have guessed it, we believe that Anne Longland is being possessed by her ancestor Maud Park Longland," Alana said.

"What are we doing about it?" Gladys asked, "Is she dangerous?"

"Anne is now under the care of the doctor and is on tranquilizers and anti-depressants, we are keeping a very close eye on her."

"Because the situation is now very serious, Queen Emelia Ray is going to come and visit, she will be having a good look around and trying to find a solution to this problem. We believe that as well as this witch's re-incarnation there is black magic going on in the village and we will be trying to get to the bottom of that," Alana said.

"But who is doing this black magic," Tina asked. She looked worried as if she was expecting this.

"We think it may be some young men but can prove nothing as yet," Jilly said.

"This is serious," Alana said, that is why the Queen will be coming to visit."

Tina looked very pale at this point. "Do you know who is responsible?" she asked. "Are they from the village?"

"We don't know at the moment," Jilly replied. "But…"

"Peter Frost's name has come up," Alana interrupted, but we don't know anything for sure."

"My Harry and Molly's Alfie were very friendly with him and so was Janice. Oh my god." Molly said. "Is there a connection?"

"It is possible," Alana said.

"I have never liked that boy he was a terrible child, always into mischief," Molly said. "He was horrendous, always wanted his own way, I never liked him playing with my Alfie. But then he was sent away to boarding school, and we did not see much of him for a few years."

"Yes, I remember we caught him stealing in the shop," Gladys said.

"The owner, old Mr Green, you remember Maurice Green, he as such a nice old chap. He contacted Lady Jane and she sorted it out, made Peter come and pay for the goods he had stolen."

"I remember old Maurice. Didn't he die unexpectantly? I remember everybody was surprised because he always seemed so robust," Tina asked.

"That is true," Molly said." The doctor said that he was fit as a fiddle it was a great shock when he died."

"We will have to keep an eye on this Peter," Alana said.

"I agree," Molly said. "When can the Queen come?"

"How are we going to explain the presence of the Queen?" Tina asked. "She might stand out in the village."

"We can say that she is a friend of mine who is visiting the area." Alana said.

"I have an idea," Molly interrupted. "Would she be willing to open the May Fair, we could say she was a famous actress of something."

"I do believe that Queen Emelia Ray would love that, "Alana said with a grin. "I will ask her."

"Well, we all have a lot to think about," David said. "But I do believe that it would be best to keep this matter quiet, so please do not mention any of this to anybody."

"Yes and no mention to Lady Jane and Meggie, we don't want to worry them until we have something concrete," Jilly said.

"Yes," Molly said. "But shouldn't Meggie know?"

"You can tell her our concerns but do not mention Peter's name, it might be a good idea to tell your children, especially Alfie to take care when he sees Peter. But try to do it so he does not suspect about the black magic stuff," Jilly paused. "By the goddess this is difficult."

"Okay I will be careful," Molly said, smiling at Jilly picking up her bag. "Can we talk tomorrow, Jilly."

"Yes, I will see you in the morning." Jilly hugged Molly, "We will get through this Molly. Don't worry."

"Everybody, take care, no carless words. We will meet again soon when I know more about the Queen's movements. "Alanna said. "Good night to you all and Blessed Be."

And with that warning the meeting broke up, they did indeed have a lot to think about, and no one more than Jilly Longland.

When Alana telephone Queen Emelia Rey to give her an update from the meeting, she asked the queen if she would mind opening the May Fair.

"I would love to," Emelia said. "It sounds like the perfect excuse and it would be fun."

"It is on May the second, opening between eleven and twelve."

"Just give me the information when I arrive."

"When will you get here?" Alana asked.

"Some time on Thursday afternoon, "Emelia Rey said. "Do you know anywhere I can stay?"

"There is a decent hotel, the Partridge Inn over in Illminster, I can give you the number."

"That's great, see you on Thursday, we will come over and have a look at your shop," the Queen said.

"That's is good. I look forward to seeing you on Thursday."

After she had spoken to the Queen, Alana sat and mused for a while. She was feeling very apprehensive.

'Emalia Rey is enjoying this,' she said to herself. 'There is a lot more going on here than we first though. I think I had better do a protection spell, to help keep the village safe.'

Alana arranged some herbs and blue candles, for peace, and recited a spell to the goddess for peace and calm and tranquility in the village.

But her appeals for quiet in the village were not to be granted, in fact things were going to get a lot worse.

Chapter thirty-three

The village 1621

Nanette and her father were working in the still room preparing herbs, in little bundles to sell. Nanette was experimenting with her cheeses and had made a goats' cheese with lavender, and some with other herbs, which were selling very well.

"A trades man has ordered fifty of the lavender goats' cheese to take to London to sell," Nanette said.

"That's wonderful," he replied distractedly.

"Are you still worrying about the river water Dad?"

"No, my sweet, but I do worry what will become of you, when I go," he said. He patted her hand as she put together the little spring of rosemary and tied them in bunches.

"Dad, I think you are going to be around a few years yet. Maybe I will have a family one day, and you can be the proud grandad, how does that sound?"

"It sounds very good. I can retire, and you and your husband and children can do all the work, while I sit back and smoke my pipe."

"You don't smoke a pipe," Nanette said.

"Maybe I will take one up," he rejoined, with a smile on his lined old face. "I would love to see you married and secure."

Teddy has never been what you would call a good-looking man, but as he aged, and his features set, he had become a distinguished looking man, with his full head of white hair and striking blue eyes.

Nanette grasped his hand and smiled back.

"I best get these done and then we can have some tea, would you like some honey cake? I made it this morning."

"I would," he answered.

Nanette released her father's hand and took up the knife and cut a bit of twine. "These are for the gypsies, she said."

Nanette resumed her task, tying the little sprigs of rosemary with a little strip of tartan ribbon. Nanette couldn't be certain but she suspected that she saw a little shine of a tear in the father's eyes, what would could bring her fathers to tears.

"What is it father? Have I upset you?"

"No," Teddy said, "you are my own sweet girl. I was just remembering your mother."

"My mother, you never talk about her,"

"You are right, when she left, I was bereft, but then I had you to look after, with the help of grandma of course. You were my world, and I pushed the lovely Demelza to the back of my mind."

"I always thought that Demelza, was a lovely name," Nanette said, please tell me about her father."

"Let us finish this task and take a break, my heart," he said, "and sit it in the sun for a while before tea."

"You look like her," he said gazing at his daughter, "but you are more, how can I say it, stable. With Demelza I always felt as she was being bound to the spot and any hard gust of wind would blow her away.

"When she left, that must have been hard for you father?"

"It was," he replied. "She was the loveliest women I have ever seen, only you match her beauty. But she was proud, from old gypsy blood, she could not be tethered to one place."

"Did you look for her?" Nanette asked.

"I made enquires, but you must remember there was little contact throughout the land, and any strangers were always under suspicion, by the authorities. These people hid themselves well, there were many fleeing from religious persecution, much as there are today. I never saw her again."

"How sad," Nanette said. She reached for his hand and held it as they watched the muted colours of the Devon countryside fade into a sunset, as it started to get cooler, they returned to their home, to have their supper.

Nanette cried that night, for the mother she had never known and for the heartbreak of her father, who had lost the only woman he had ever loved.

Chapter thirty-four

The village, 17th century

Rituals were held at the old Altar Stone in the village, every so often at the Spring Equinox and the Winter Equinox, and All Saints Eve and Beltane. Nanette had not become involved in these rituals, until after the incident with the brook, and Nanette's part in making sure the village could still get clean water.

But one day an elder in the village approached Nanette and asked if she would like to join her group.

"We are few, and we are very careful, these are dangerous times," the woman said, "But we need to stand together."

"But Sonia. What is it that you do?"

"Nothing much really we worship nature and pray for good harvests, an easy birth, that sort of thing, but we do it together." Sonia looked worried. "It must be kept secret, you know what is going on in this realm, with King James's men rampaging through the country looking for anyone they can persecute. We are trusting you, and that is why I come to you Nanette," Sonia paused. "Do you want to join us?"

"Are you witches?" Nanette whispered hardly daring to say the word out loud.

"We practice the old ways; we are women of the craft."

"What craft?" Nanette asked, "my father is an herbalist he makes poppets and remedies, is that the craft?"

"Yes. In a way, it is and there are many men who have the talent, you are doubly blessed, because of your father and your gypsy mother," Sonia stated. "We know you have talent we see it in the way the animals love you and your way with making beautiful thing, you are at one with nature," Sonia, said. "Do you not know it? Nanette."

"I think I do," Nanette replied. "I have always been able to get close to living creatures even as a child. And I love all my animals, and know them all individually, I hate it if one has to die. My father always takes over that job."

Nanette had always known that she could get her own way, change peoples will, she had used this to sell her cheeses and other products, luring people to look and then buy.

They agreed to meet at the Altar Stone for the next meeting.

 "It must be in secret," Sonia said.

"Why must it be in secret, are we in danger?"

"We are always in danger, my girl, there are those among us who would do us harm." Sonia paused and stared into Nanette's eyes, "We are trusting you in this, or we would not ask you to join us."

"I will be discreet," Nanette said. "I will never reveal your secret."

Sonia nodded. "Good," she said. "Do you know your family history?"

"Yes, a little, but grandma does not like to talk about it."

"There have been two women in your family that have been executed by the authorities as witches, did you know that?" Sonia asked.

"Yes, I did," Nanette replied. "Grandma, told me, she was always saying that I must always be careful, and not bring attention to myself."

"Good advice, we were worried. Your confrontation with the Frost family over the water rights issue, but talk seems to have died down. But we must still execute great discretion in all out works, and not give anyone a chance to call us out, you do understand?"

"I do," Nanette said solemnly. "I promise that I will never betray you."

On the next full moon Nanette was welcomed into the village coven.

The ladies met at the Altar Stone, in the past these ceremonies would have been held sky clad, but in this village the women simply needed to have bathed and wear clean clothes.

"We meet this night my goddess to ask for your help," Sonia said, as she lit the candles and placed flowers in the center of the Altar Stone, where they all stood in a circle holding hands. Sonia stood in the middle and she held a quartz wand, an ancient artifact that was used in rituals to the moon. This one had come down though the families for hundreds of years.

"We ask for your protection in these hazardous times when men seek to persecute us. Please watch over our member Hilda, may she delivery her baby safely and keep mother and child secure under your protection. May the harvest be good and bring us rain to help the crops grow strong, and lastly please welcome our new member Nanette Longland to our group."

Nanette had dressed in a long white dress and she had woven some summer flowers into her hair. She stepped forward and Sonia took her hands.

"Will you promise to be loyal and true to the ways of the Mother Goddess?"

"I will."

"Will you support and respect us and keep our rituals and live secret and close to your heart?"

"I will."

"Then Nanette Longland, we welcome you to the coven, together my we protect out village from harm."

"Blessed be," the entire group rejoined. "Welcome Nanette, we are many and we are as one."

When the ceremony was done Nanette felt for the first time completely in accord with the women of the village.

Chapter thirty-five

The village early 17th century.

In 1642 the English civil war started. In the village young men were recruited to fight, and many lost their lives.

Nanette found herself in a world plagued by the witch hunters. James the First had written his book Demonology, which actually sought to prevent the wrongful conviction of witchcraft. But because most of the populace could not read, its intention was ignored and the persecution of so called, witches was as fervent as ever.

Nanette had married, a local man called Benjamin. He was a good man and tolerant of the ways of the village women, with their herbs and potions, but he became nervous when the witchfinders started to circulate the country. Nanette had done well, and her business had prospered and at the age of forty-five she had three grandchildren by her son Frederick and his wife Mary.

"We must take great care," Benjamin said. "I have heard stories that in Exeter three women were hanged."

"We are careful husband," Nanette said. "Eat up your pottage," she said to her grandsons, "look Jane has emptied her bowl."

"People, become envious," he said, "please, don't dismiss my warning."

"I won't my sweet, I will be watchful."

Little Thomas was kicking his brother, Willy, under the table and fidgeting. He wanted to go and run outside to play with his friends. "They are like little wild things," Benjamin said.

"Yes, Mary has her hands full there's no doubt," Nanette said. "Off you go then," she said to the boys.

And they were up and out the door before she could blink.

"What about you my little princess what do you want to do today?" Nanette asked Jane.

"Can I help you with the herbs and can you teach me more about the remedies and potions you make?" Jane asked, "and can I take little Salty with us?"

"I don't see how we can stop him, as he follows you everywhere you go, even to your bed."

The farm cat had had kittens and one little mite, a tiny ball of black and white fluff, had adopted little Jane and he never left her side.

"There's no doubt that she is a Longland," Nanette's husband said. "She has inherited all that love for nature from you, my dove," Benjamin joked. "I had better watch out."

Nanette smiled at her husband. "You just keep an eye on those boys, until their Ma and Pa geta back from Illminster."

"I'll get them to help me feed the goats, they will like that," he replied.

"Good idea," Nanette said, "Come on my little love, let us go pick some herbs; rosemary, thyme and lavender for the possets, we are going to make."

There was still some conflict with the Longland family and the

Frost estate, but relations had been much better while Piers was the new Lord Frost. But there were other families in the district that, knew they could make money from the persecution of the Hedge wives or Cunning folk as they were sometimes called.

One such was the hosteler, Tobias, of the Partridge Inn over in Illminster. He had a grievance against women, after his wife ran off.

He reported his wife and her sister for putting a curse on him, and his wife Oriana had gone to stay in Little Barnstead with her sister Jackeline. And Jackeline was a member of Nanette's women's group.

Tobias stated that she had performed, with her sister, a spell to make him impotent, and he reported them as witches.

"She put a spell on me," he recounted to the local magistrate, "she made me, I can hardly say the word, impotent, and then she mocked me when I could not perform, "Tobias, said. "The witch and her sister did this."

"The truth is that Tobias is a sot and his impotence is the result of his excessive drinking," Oriana, related to Nanette, "he regularly got drunk tried to have sex with me and would then beat me when he could not perform, and that I why I left."

"This is not an unusual story; men always blame someone else for their own misfortunes and inadequacies."

"Can we hide her?" Jackeline asked, "they will come here, but I don't know where to go."

"Take this and go to a big town, Bristol or even London, you can hide more easily in a crowd, hopefully they will not try to follow you."

Nanette gave the sisters some money and they hired a cart to take them north and out of danger.

Oriana had managed to hide in her sister's house, and when the officers from the magistrate came to arrest them, the sisters had gone.

The villagers were questioned relentlessly about the sisters and their whereabouts.

"I know nothing of their location, "Grandma Longland said, "they were here, but then one morning they had gone. We do not know where they went."

"We didn't know Jackeline well, "Nanette added, "and I did not know her sister. I have never met her."

The government men badgered the women of the village for nearly a week but could find no proof that the villagers had helped the couple escape. It was a great relief when they saw the questioners' leave.

"We must be doubly careful," Nanette, "we are in their sights now and they will not let this rest."

"Yes, we must not do anything to bring their attention back to the village," Benjamin said.

"Indeed, the country is aflame with the witchfinder zeal. I have heard news of this Witchfinder General, who is responsible for hundreds of deaths in Essex, they say he is paid by the head," Nanette said.

"What a despicable man," Benjamin said. "You would think that the King, would have done more to stop this religious persecution, but it seems that he has just made matters worse."

"We live in dangerous times," Nanette replied, "and we must be very careful."

Two months went by before the militia men returned, this time they came straight to the door of Nanette Longland.

"We have reason to believe that you are practicing witchcraft," "one man said. "You are required to come with us."

As Nanette was escorted outside a crowd appeared, Nanette's husband came running up from the farm, but he was held back by two villagers.

The local priest was there, and a crowd of men around him, like a flock of ugly birds.

"There she is," he shouted. "Never comes to church and my wife … wife, "he stuttered, "my own wife has purchased her poppets and herbs."

"This is true," one woman shouted, "she does magic, I have seen it."

"What have you seen woman?" one of the men asked," as he dragged Nanette toward an old cart.

"She can affect the weather. I witnessed her saying 'let it rain,' and the next moment the sky darkened, and rain fell on the village."

All this commotion warned Mary, Nanette's daughter in law, and she also came running. But could not get close because a crowd had assembled, and they were now baying for blood outside the church.

Mary saw Nanette being pulled from the cart and dragged into the church house, but the mob was pushing and gathering and she could not get any nearer, she stopped by the old yew tree that grew in the cemetery in next to the church.

An old woman in an apron crowed to a companion. "They'll find out now, they'll see the mark of the witch."

Mary stepped out from behind the branches of the tree and stared at the woman in shock.

"What did you say?" she demanded, "what mark of the witch?"

The old woman cackled, a vicious sound the tightened Mary's stomach. "Don't you know?" she cried with glee. "All witches have and extra teat! They hide it under their clothes."

"Why do you say that?" Mary demanded, but weakly, her legs would barely hold her. Sonia put her hand on Mary's shoulder.

"Say no more, it will betray us all. Nanette will say nothing, we must allow her that."

Then Nanette was being dragged out of the church house.

"We have a witch," the man shouted. "She has the mark."

"They have found a mark," the priest said, "and she has a bag full of the devil's tools."

"What have you found?" one village man shouted.

"She has a bag with herbs, stones, a lock of hair and what looks like nail clippings," The priest answered. "Tis devil's work.

"What has she done?" one woman asked, "She is a good woman and she helps people. She has helped us all at one time or another, and while the war took away our men."

"Shut your mouth you dirty old hag, or do you want to join her?" one of the arresting men snarled.

"No," the old woman said, backing away in terror.

Nanette was thrown roughly into the cart, two men held her fast, and they were driven away.

"We go to the assizes in Exeter, "one of them called.

Mary turned away and retched, bringing up her dinner on the sacred green grass of the graveyard.

"How could this happen?" she cried.

As the cart pulled away the people of the village were suddenly silent and started to wander off in a trance, as if they did not know what had happened.

"Nanette had been a good neighbour, she had often helped the people of the village," one woman said.

"She was kind and helpful to me, when my husband died," one elderly woman was heard to say, "What happened here?"

"They found a witch," a man said, turning with a look of confusion to his wife.

"But she was our friend," his wife responded.

The people of the village were stunned and could not believe what had happened. It was as if a frenzy of resentment suddenly overtook them, and now they could not explain their actions.

On the edge of the crowd, keeping to himself was Piers Frost, he watched as Nanette was driven away and then turned on his horse to return to his home.

Two weeks later Nanette was found guilty at the Exeter court house, and she was subsequently hanged by the neck until dead.

Even though she was starved, abused and tortured, they could not get Nanette to admit to witchcraft or name anybody in the village.

She never spoke one single word to anybody from the day she was arrested.

Chapter thirty-six

It was a gloriously sunny spring day when Queen Emelia Rey arrived in Little Barnstead. It caused quite a stir. Her Rolls Royce pulled up outside Pandoras Box and Emelia Rey and Hermosa climbed out. The Witch Queen was dressed in a startling midnight blue dress and jacket covered in thousands of shinny jet stones, with shoes and bag to match. Hermosa echoed her mistress in a paler blue outfit which was a little subtler and Kigali was in a sharp dark blue suit and black shirt.

"So, this is your little shop," Emelia said, "how lovely.

Emelia and Hermosa strode into the shop and looked around.

"Where did you find all these lovely things?" Hermana asked picking up one of Jilly's statues. "Look your majesty, these figures are wonderful."

"I just love these candles, who makes them?" Emelia asked. "And I'll have this little silver charm for Ebony's collar. And the dreamcatchers, are divine. I must have this one," Emelia plucked from the display a bright blue hanging mobile with silver stars and cobweb design. "It is so beautiful."

Alana was expecting the Queen, but she was still taken aback at the imperious magnificence of her actually being there, and she was overwhelmed by the questions being hurled at her from Emelia and Hermosa.

"Welcome, welcome, can I get you something to drink? I have elderberry wine. I know you like that."

"How kind, we will not be here long. I want to eat out in a little restaurant we have found in Illminster," Emelia said. "Would you like to join us?"

"Why, yes, I would … I would love to," Alana stuttered. "What is the name?"

"No worries, Kigali will pick you up at say seven tonight, is that okay?"

"That would be great," Alana replied.

In all this time Emelia had been adding to a pile goods on the counter, from all over the shop.

"And those silver candles, Hermosa, for the Aqua sitting room, don't you think?" Emelia said. "And the gold ones too and the pink with the silver filigree design. Where do you get this stuff?" Emelia demanded.

At that moment Jilly came into the shop, she had seen the Rolls Royce and Kigali standing by the door, but she still stopped in shock when she saw Emelia Rey and Hermosa.

"This is my friend Jilly Longland," Alana said quickly. "It is her that alerted us to the situation in the village. Jilly this is the Witch Queen Emelia Rey and her companion Hermosa."

"Very pleased to meet you," Jilly said, making a quick curtsy.

"No need for that," The Queen said holding out her hand. "We don't go in for all that sycophantic stuff, nice to meet you."

That caused Hermosa to raise an eyebrow, when she glanced up at Alana, but she quickly returned to examining the stock in the shop.

"My Queen what do you think of these figures?" Hermosa asked.

"But they are splendid, so earthy," the Queen responded. "Who makes them?"

"I do," Jilly replied meekly, somewhat taken aback.

"You do?" How wonderful, can I commission a large one for my Chelsea Garden? Can you do that?"

"Well, yes if you let me know what size you want and I can give you a quote," Jilly said. "You can let me have the details, or I can get them via Alana."

Jilly had noticed that the Queen did not have a long attention span and was now looking at the dream catchers again.

"Where do you get all these beautiful things? Alana."

"Well, I have many contacts in the witchy world and I have found some wonderful local people, like for the candles and essential oils."

"We will take a few of these as well Hermosa. Do you have neroli? It is so hard to find in London."

"Yes, and plain orange," Alana picked up a small bottle and showed it to Emelia.

"Get three of each, will you Hermosa," the Queen said.

"About the May Fair," Jilly asked.

"Just tell Alana where and when I have to be there, okay."

The Queen was sipping her cordial and then she looked up at Jilly, "You are the witches relative?" she suddenly said.

"Yes, I am Jilly Longland, but I did not know much about my

infamous relatives, until this year."

"Well, isn't that something." The Queen said. "Hermosa pay for everything will you? We will be off in a minute or two."

"Yes, your majesty," Hermosa said.

"So, tell me Jilly, what is going on with your sister? Anne, isn't it?"

"We think that she is being possessed by Maud Longland, she has been acting very strangely for a few weeks now," Jill explained. "I have called the doctor and she is on tranquilizers; she hardly leaves the house anymore."

"This all very interesting," Emelia stopped talking and just stared at Jilly, for what seemed like several minutes, looking deep into her eyes.

"Shopping is ready to go," Hermosa said. "I will call Kigali to put it in the car."

"Yes, you do that," Emelia said, not taking her eyes off Jilly.

When Hermosa and Kigali, left the shop arms full of purchases, the Queen turned to Alana.

"See you later then, goodbye Jilly. Alana you can bring Jilly tonight?" Emelia said and then she was gone.

"Wow," Jilly said when the door shut, and the Rolls Royce pulled away. "I think she was actually inside my head."

"She does that." Alana looked in a state of shock. "I have just taken more money in the last few minutes, than I have since I came to live here."

"What a woman, the villagers won't know what hits them on Saturday," Jilly remarked.

When Emelia and her assistants left the shop, they found that a small group of people had gathered outside. Emelia smiled and waved at them as she was carried away, in her wonderful car.

"Who is she?" one of lady asked.

"Some famous film star," answered another.

"I think that was Emelia Rey," Tina said. "She is so beautiful."

"Emelia Rey, I heard that she was going to open the May Fair on Saturday," a woman said.

"Yes," Tina said, "she is."

"Wow, that will be great. I must tell my friends," The woman enthused. "What films has she been in?"

"I don't know," Tina said. "I'm not much for the cinema myself, but I understand that she is rather famous in Hollywood."

"Really?" the woman said, "I can't wait to see her again on Saturday."

"What do we know about this Emelia Rey?" Jim asked Brenda as they were having breakfast Thursday morning.

"She is an actress." Brenda replied, "a film star.

"I have never heard of her," Jim retorted.

"When was the last time you went to see a film?"

"Good point, but we don't know anything about her."

"Molly says that she is very beautiful, and that she is visiting friends in Illminster, and that she is willing to open the May Fair, for free, what else do we need to know?"

"How does Molly know this famous film star?" Jim asked cynically.

"Molly said that she is a friend of Alana," Brenda replied. "Look we should be grateful, she will draw a crowd and we can't afford to pay some celebrity to come down from London, can we?"

"I just don't like not knowing anything about her, but I take your point, we don't have anyone else."

"Are you ready for tonight?" Brenda asked. "Do you have your service planned and the timetable ready? What time are the choristers coming? I have arranged some finger food and I am going to make a fruit punch for the refreshments."

"Yes, it is all in hand, Father Jack will come over an hour earlier so we can agree the format for the service, and we will commence the program at seven in the evening."

"Good, I am going to drive into Exeter today and get a few bits and pieces for Saturday. What are you doing today?" Brenda asked.

"I have a few things to attend to, but I will be back mid-afternoon."

"Good, see you later then," Brenda said as she finished her tea and toast and left to go and get ready to go out.

"I wonder what he is really doing," she said to herself, "as if I care."

Brenda was meeting Andy and they were going out for lunch, in town.

"Two of us can play this game," Brenda said. "I deserve a life too."

Chapter thirty-seven

Brenda was right to wonder what Jim was up to, he was in fact going to see his friend Jeremey.

"Has it come?" Jim said as soon as the door opened.

"Nice to see you too," Jeremy said. "Do come in."

"Sorry, I am just so excited."

Jeremy produced a large flat parcel and handed it over to Jim. "There you go, arrived yesterday."

Jim took the parcel over to the table and looked at Jeremy with an expression of jubilation and fear in his eyes.

"What if it doesn't fit?" he said.

"You won't know until you open it," Jeremy said, he was now looking on in expectation. "Go on I am dying to see."

Jim tentatively remover the outer layer of brown paper to find a large pink and white stripped box. "I can't," he said.

"Open the bloody thing, now," Jeremy nearly screamed.

"Okay, okay, no need to shout."

Jim slowly removed the lid of the box, pulled aside some tissue paper and then his mouth flew open.

"Oh my," Jim gasped. "It's just…"

Inside the box was the most beautiful dress, it was a pale lilac with tinny purple embroidered flower buds all over it, there were stunning see-through sleeves that ended at the elbow with a lilac velvet cuff.

"Get it out, let's have a look," Jeremy said. "That is spectacular. Quickly Jim, try it on."

Jim divested himself of his outer clothing in seconds and picked up the amazing dress, he looked at Jeremy in awe.

"I can't believe it."

Jim slipped the fantastic creation over his head and did up the side zip, it fitted perfectly.

"It's wonderful, look how the colours change when you move, Jeremy said, "and the shoes and gloves. Come on now I want to see the complete transformation."

"Jim gasped as he looked in the mirror.

"I need my wig and then some make up."

"Goodbye to Jim and welcome to Jaqueline, you will look stunning."

"You are going to be the belle of the ball," Jeremy said. "Do you want to leave the dress and accessories here until the party or will you take it home?" Jeremy stood admiring the outfit. "Such a shame that you are so much slimmer than me or I would be tempted to put it on myself."

Jeremy was going to have a party for his friends and the local transvestite crowd, and Jim had ordered this dress for that occasion.

"I think I will take it home. I will have to hide it from Brenda, but that should not be a problem," Jim said. "I want to wear in the shoes a bit before the party."

"As you wish," Jeremy said. "How is your wife?"

"I think she is having an affair," Jim said.

"No, really?"

"Yes, I cannot blame her really, and we are just running along together, but I think she is reaching breaking point," Jim said. "I will not be surprised if she plans to leave me soon."

"Do you ever, you know… have sex?" Jeremy asked.

"No, we have separate rooms and rarely share the same bed."

"Do you know who she is having an affair with?"

"Yes, it is our local handy man, Andy, she has been spending a lot of time with him," Jim paused, "but when we are all together, in company, she pointedly avoids him."

"Does anybody else know?"

"I would not be surprised, it is pretty obvious," Jim said.

"And you, how do you feel about this?"

"I know deep down that I cannot continue to live my life as a lie, it has to end. Perhaps our separating will be the turning point."

"I think you are right, you need to live your life, but if you are not a priest, what will you do?" Jeremy asked.

"I am not sure, but I will find something."

Brenda had picked up some supplies in Exeter before meeting up with Andy in a local hotel. He was seated in the foyer when she arrived and jumped to his feet to greet her.

"There you are my darling. I was starting to worry that you were not coming."

"It took longer than I thought at the catering store, I needed some things for tomorrow."

"Are we all set now?" he asked.

"What we don't have now, we won't have," Brenda said grimly.

"Meggie, Jilly and Molly and possible Anne are all making food, we should have enough to sell on the day. I just hope it doesn't rain."

"I would not count on anything much from Anne, from what Jilly told me she is somewhat comatose, and moves around in a daze most of the time."

"You saw Jilly?" Brenda asked.

"She is just a friend, Brenda," he said taking her hand, "you are my world now, but Jilly is still a friend."

"I know, I hate this sneaking around."

"Not for much longer," Andy said. "Let's go eat, I hear that they do a good buffet in this hotel, and I am starving. I have booked a room?"

"That was a bit presumptuous of you," she said with a grin.

"Was I wrong?" Andy asked.

"No, you are a naughty," Brenda said. "But you were not wrong."

Chapter thirty-eight

In the dress shop, Tina had been tutoring Sofie in the art of repairs and dress making for quite a few months.

"You are doing very well," Tina said one morning. "Would like to do an order all by yourself?"

"Do you think I am ready?" Sofie asked.

"It is a simple over tunic, for Jilly. I think you are more than ready, and it would leave me free to work on the bridesmaid's dresses for that lady in Smalltown."

"Okay, I will do a good job for you Tina," Sofie said. "I promise."

Sofie had found that she really enjoyed working with all the lovely materials, and helping to do measuring and preparation work, she longed to work on her own commission.

"She is a changed girl," Molly said to Tina when they met in the grocers. "She has really buckled down to this job. I am so glad. We did worry about her."

"She is a great help to me and works hard. I really think that she has a talent for design. I allowed her to make herself a dress with some material left from an order that got cancelled, it turned out quite beautifully."

"Yes, she showed me," Molly said, "that must have been very expensive fabric, shot silk, was it? And such a beautiful colour. It was so nice of you to let her have it."

"It was an experiment, and Sofie passed with flying colours. I can trust her to do work on her own now."

"That's wonderful, and I must say it does help having another wage coming in," Molly said. "Things are a bit tight at the moment, what with Alfie at university."

"Do you know that Sofie is seeing my Harry?" Tina asked. "I think it is quite innocent, at the moment. He often stops to chat with her at work and has taken her out at lunchtime for a walk on the green, although I discourage it. But I do think there is something growing between them."

"We do know, I think she has quite a crush on him."

"So, you are okay with it?"

"Yes, I think he is a nice boy," Molly said.

"Are those boys still getting together? I like your Alfie, but that Peter is trouble if you ask me," Tina said. "I think he is a bad influence on the other boys, and after what was said at the meeting. I am now very uncomfortable that he is hanging around with Harry and Alfie."

"I agree. Bert did have a talk with Alfie about it," Molly said. "But Alfie said that he did not know what all the fuss was. Peter is fun and he has money and he buys them drinks. I still think that he eggs them on to behave badly."

"I hope he just goes away again soon. He will have to go back to his work?" Tina said. "How are your preparations for the May Fair going?" Tina asked.

"I am on top of it, I think we will be ready," Molly replied. "You?"

"I have made quite a lot of things and Sofie has helped a lot. She has come up with some wonderful ideas for things to sell. I am going to give her a half share of the profit on what we take at the Fair."

"That is kind of you, I am sure she will be very grateful." Molly smiled. "Have you heard that Emelia Rey is coming down from London, she is going to open the May Fair."

"Yes, you mentioned it at the meeting."

"Of course. I am that excited," Molly said. "I think it will draw in a few more people."

"That's good. I am so looking forward to meeting her, Alana does not tell us much, but I think she is very powerful and extremely good looking from what I have heard."

"Yes, we must hope that she can clear up this mess."

" Well, yes, be seeing you," Tina replied getting ready to move on.

"Wait. Did you hear about Anne?" Molly said.

"Yes," Tina said. "I understand that she has had some kind of breakdown."

"Yes, she attacked Alana with a knife," Molly said, "and then passed out on to the floor, when she woke up, she was very disorientated. Jilly managed to get her home and then phoned the doctor and she has to stay in bed a few days and he has prescribed antidepressants and tranquilizers."

"That terrible, but she has been acting very strangely for the past few weeks," Tina said.

"I am helping Jilly keep an eye on her when I go in on the mornings, she has been very subdued since her attack on Alana, and she just keeps to her room," Molly said, "and now Jilly stays in the house more often than usual, to keep an eye on Anne."

"It is all very worrying," Tina said.

"Let us hope that the Queen can sort this all out," Molly said in excitement.

"Yes, I am so glad that I had the idea for her to open the May Fair, we are saying that she is famous actress from Hollywood."

"I think it is going to be wonderful day," Molly said. "I do hope nothing goes wrong. We have all worked so hard to get everything organized."

"Yes, I am looking forward to it," Tina said. "I know the children are excited, the local school has been making fancy dresses. I gave the school a few off cuts of material and ribbons." Tina paused. "I think it will be good for the village, wake us all up a bit."

"That was nice of you." Molly smiled. "You are right my lot are so excited, and so am I.""

Anne was proud as a peacock that it was on her initiative that Emelia Rey was going to open the May Fair.

"It's going to be wonderful." Molly couldn't contain her excitement. "I just can't wait, our own May Fair, again after all these years.

Tina shook her head as she watched Molly's excited face with amusement. "I am sure everything will go marvelously.

Chapter thirty-nine

Peter and Alfie were seated in the corner of the local pub.

"I have decided to do wealth and prosperity ritual on the eve of May Day before the fair," Peter said quietly. "We will do a magic ritual for property and a sacrifice, are you up for it?"

"What about Harry?" Are you going to ask him?" Alfie asked. "Or maybe Andy? Do we need make up a four?"

"Well, we know that Andy has become too absorbed in the village ladies, especially now he his bonking the vicar's wife, so he is out," Peter said.

"Andy is bonking Brenda? Are you sure?" Alfie asked.

"Everybody knows, where have you been?"

"Nobody, told me. Andy and Brenda having an affair, oh my, I wonder if Father Jim knows." Alfie said.

"They always say the husband is the last to know," Peter said. "I will speak with Harry. I would like him to bring Sofie," Peter continued.

"I don't think that she will not want to be involved."

"Harry will bring her, if I tell him to."

"She would make up the four," Alfie said. "Will my sister be, okay? I don't like bringing her in to this."

"Yes, we won't need them for long. It will be fine Alfie. It will be fine!" Peter repeated.

"You are sure? Alfie asked.

"Yes," Peter replied, looking deep into Alfie's eyes. "IT WILL BE FINE."

Alfie felt woozy for a few seconds and then he was back again.

"Why do we need to do this spell again, you are doing alright aren't you?" Alfie asked. "A nice car and a god job?"

"For more money," Peter said.

"But you already have a lot of money and you will inherit Frost House."

"There is never too much money," Peter replied. "Don't you do know that?

Alfie nodded. "Okay, see you later," Alfie said. "But I still don't understand why…"

"Just do as I ask," Peter snapped back at Alfie, "see you later.

"Yes, Peter," Alfie mumbled.

When Alana and Jilly were picked up to go and have a meal with Emelia Rey, they had no idea where they were going.

"You look stunning," Alana said when they met outside Pandoras Box just before seven o'clock.

"So, do you," Jilly replied. "What amazing colours."

Both ladies had pulled out all the stops. Jilly's was in a smart but elegant dress and jacket in a striking black and yellow print.

Alana was in a free-flowing caftan like dress of multi colours, a linen/silk mix which seemed alive as she moved. Jilly had put her curly hair up and it was kept in place by two beautiful mother of pearl combs.

"Do you know where we are going?" Jilly asked.

"I have no idea," Alana replied, "but if I know the Queen it will be somewhere spectacular."

At that moment Kigali pulled up in the Rolls and then they were on their way.

As they drove along, through country roads, Jilly still had no idea where they were going to.

"Where are we heading for?" she asked Kigali.

"It is a little country house, we will be there soon," he replied.

They turned down what looked like an overgrown lane and pulled up in front of a small but exquisite little thatched house.

Standing regally on the steps were Emelia Rey and Hermosa.

"Welcome, don't you both look lovely," Emelia gushed, as she rushed forward to greet them. "Come this way."

Emelia Rey was dressed in a stunningly simple crimson silk shift dress, and an exquisite gold necklace of rubies and gold links, with ear pendants to match, she looked amazing.

Hermosa hustled them into the house which had suddenly taken on the appearance of the swishiest looking modern restaurant. There was a round table set for five people and dressed in the finest linen and tableware.

"Come sit next to me," Emelia said to Jilly. "I want to find out all about you."

At that moment a very short man with a bald head and large ears walked in the room. He was wearing chefs clothing, including a tall hat that seemed perched on top of his dome like head, resting on his ears. He came straight over and addressed the Queen.

"Are you ready for the first course, your majesty?" he asked.

"Please, give us a moment to get settled," the Queen said. "This is Bruno, he is a great friend of mine and a wizard with food. I think we are in for a treat."

Bruno bowed to Emelia Rey and said, "It will be my pleasure to serve your most magnificent highness and her worthy guests."

Hermosa grinned at Jilly and pulled out a chair for her to sit next to the Queen.

Bruno put a wine cooler on the table containing a bottle of white wine, there was also a bottle of a red wine standing open on a nearby trolly.

"Kigali would you serve the wine?" Bruno asked, before he disappeared again back into the kitchen.

"It would be my pleasure," Kigali answered and promptly poured out a glass of white wine for everybody.

"I forgot to ask, "Emelia said. "Do you have any allergies?"

"I can't eat celery or peanuts," Jilly said.

"Kigali, please go and tell Bruno no celery or peanuts, would you?"

"Yes, my Queen." Kigali was back a minute later. "No problem, but Bruno asked if we are ready for the first course?"

"Yes," Emelia said.

Hermosa and Kigali had joined the party and when everyone was comfortably seated, Bruno returned with five bowls of cold grape soup. The soup had a swirl of fresh cream on the top and was garnished with tiny little sweet green grapes and thin slices of kiwi fruit.

Jilly took a spoon full. "This is heaven," she said. "Who would have thought of a starter like this."

"Bruno is very cleaver at experimenting with different foods,"

The soup was followed by a delicious chicken liver pate, and a green herb salad.

"So, Jilly please tell me something about yourself," Emelia said.

"There's not a lot to tell. I have a sister as you know, Anne, and we have lived in the village our entire lives," Jilly began. "But I never knew much about our history or anything about our ancestors."

"Your family is well known in the Witch chronicles, and it would seem that one of your ancestors is causing a lot of trouble at the moment?"

"You mean this, Maud Park Longland. Alana thinks that she is taking over Anne's mind," Jilly said.

"It would seem so," Emelia said. "Maud Park Longland was a very powerful hedge witch and came from a long line of gifted people. Her mother and her daughter were accused of witchcraft and they both died horribly."

"How dreadful, and I had no idea," Jilly shuddered. "Anne has always been what we used call whimsical. As a child she was always being told to grow up and stop imagining things."

"That must have made her feel very frustrated, it is no wonder that emotions built up inside her. She was like a ticking bomb," Emelia Rey said.

Jilly shuddered and went very pale as she looked down at her empty plate.

"I am sorry, Jilly, this must be very hard for you?"

"It is all a bit overwhelming."

Alana was talking to Hermosa, but every few minutes she looked over at Jilly, and seemed to be getting a bit annoyed at Emelia Rey for monopolizing Jilly in conversation.

"I am very interested in your sculptures," Emelia said, "and I do want to commission one for my Chelsea Garden project."

"That would be great. If you let me know which figure you want and the size. I will get back to you with a quote," Jilly said.

Bruno re-appeared to take the plates and then bring them all a small lemon sorbet, garnished with crystalized mint leaves, to cleanse their taste buds in readiness of the main course.

Kigali got up to pour the red wine ready for the meat dish, and he smiled at Jilly as be topped up her glass.

"Thank you," Jilly said smiling up Kigali.

He was an impressive figure of a man; his skin was so dark that his teeth and the whites of his dark eyes shone brightly in contrast.

Kigali winked at Jilly before sitting down again and chatting to Alana, trying to distract Alana from her avid surveillance of the Queen and Jilly.

"I will have to have a look at your sculptures and then we can decide," Emelia said. "It will be nice to see your workshop."

"I can help you there…" Alana started to say, but she was interrupted by the arrival of the next course, perfectly cooked slices of roast beef, rolled and stuffed with truffles, accompanied by mixture of spring vegetables.

It was quiet for a few minutes as they ate their meal, and when knives and forks were put aside.

"Have you thought about what you are going to do when this matter is sorted out?" Hermosa asked Alana.

"What?" Alana asked, her attention was still concentrated on Jilly, who was still deep in conversation with Emelia Rey.

"Are you going to stay here with Jilly?" Hermosa said. "You two have grown very close, I think."

"No, I mean yes," Alana struggled to understand what Hermosa was saying.

"Yes," Emelia Rey suddenly said, joining the general conversation. "Do you want to stay here, in the village?"

"I don't know," Alana said, and then her eyes met with Jilly's, and something happened, a sudden look of understanding went between them. "Yes, I do think I might stay hereabouts."

Alana was saved from further embarrassment, by the re-emergence of Bruno with one more delicate sorbet, passion fruit this time with two perfectly delicate raspberries on the side.

This was followed by the fish course, a creamy white fish in a tantalizing lemon sauce served with tiny shell shaped pasta.

Bruno is truly a genius," Kigali said. "More wine anybody?" he asked.

"Yes please, I have never had such a meal," Jilly said, trying to change the subject away from Alana, who she could see was in a little bit agitated.

"Do you have other houses as well as the one in London," she asked Emelia Rey, by way of changing the subject of the conversation.

"Why, yes, my dear, you must come and visit sometime. I have an adorable little villa on Lake Como, in Italy. But of course, I have many friends who would put me up at any time, all over the world."

"How wonderful," Jilly said.

"Have you traveled much my dear?" Emelia asked.

"No, I haven't, but I would love to see more of the world," Jilly answered. "And I have always wanted to go to Italy."

Bruno returned a few minutes later with the deserts, a mango fool, so creamy and delicious that there was silence for a few minutes, this was followed by cheese and biscuits.

Bruno returned when they had all finished to take the plates, and then he carried in a tray with some brandy and tiny little sweet crisp wafers.

"I hope you all enjoyed your meal?" he asked.

"We most certainly have," Emelia Rey said. And everybody clapped the little man, who turned a bright pink, but seem very happy.

"My pleasure your majesty, it has been an honor to serve you and your guests."

After they had drunk some brandy and chatted for a while, the party started getting ready to leave.

"Kigali will give you two a lift home, and I will see you tomorrow, Alana. We need to get together to discuss what is going on here in Little Barnstead."

"Yes," Alana said. "Will you come to the shop of shall I meet you at your hotel?"

"I will come to the shop, and I want to have another look around the village, and see some of Jilly's sculptures, so I can decide which one I want to commission."

"Goodbye," Jilly said as they walked to the car. "It has been a pleasure. I will never forget that meal it was … it was well amazing."

"He is a treasure, that is for sure. See you tomorrow, Jilly," The Queen touched Jilly's hand and, she felt a tingle and surge of warmth go through her body.

"Yes, your majesty," Jilly said breathlessly.

"Now … now, none of that, call me Emelia."

The Queen then turned to Alana. "See you in the morning."

Then she watched as the car pulled away.

"That went well," Hermosa said.

"Indeed, it was fascinating," Emelia Rey replied. "I am looking forward to this May Fair, it could be fun."

"Yes, I think it will be very interesting." Hermosa replied as she watched the car disappearing into the night.

"What on earth shall I wear?" The Queen mussed.

"Oh, I am sure we can throw something together, "Hermosa said with a grin.

"You will have to give me directions Jilly's house. I know how to get back to the village. But I don't know where your home is," Kigali said.

"That's fine," Jilly replied. "Go to the village and I will direct you from there."

As Jilly and Alana settled in the back of the car, Alana reached out and took Jilly's hand, and Jilly squeezed it in return.

When Jilly directed Kigali to her house and it just seemed natural for Alana to get out there too.

"Is this okay for you?" Kigali asked Alana.

"Yes, it is not far to my flat, I can walk from here.

Jilly and Alana stood together in the road, and watched the big car disappear.

"Is something happening here?" Jilly asked.

"I think so, is that okay with you?"

"I think you had better come in and I will make some coffee," Jill said. "What an amazing meal."

Alana stood back and gazed at Jilly.

"Are we going to talk about it?" Alana said pointedly reaching to touch Jilly's cheek.

Jilly smiled, and then she opened her arms, and Alana stepped into them.

"This is not something that I have expected to happen to me again," Jilly said.

"Nor me, but I am glad that it has," Alana said. And then she took Jilly's face in her hands and kissed her, then stepped back and smiled.

"Can we just take is slowly," Jilly said. "I do have a lot going on at the moment."

"I will take it any way you want," Alana said. "Slowly is good for me, my darling. I think that I will go home now."

"Not too slowly," Jilly said, and smiled back at Alana.

Then they parted, and Alana walked home. Jilly watched as Alana disappeared down the road.

'What a night,' she thought. 'My world is changing beyond belief. And I thought this mission was going to be boring.'

Chapter forty

1st May 1959 at the Altar Stone

"I don't think they will come," Alfie said. "Harry is too spooked by what he remembers and even more spooked by what he has forgotten."

Peter had told Alfie to ask Harry and Sofie, to come to their ritual on the Friday night. Alfie had spoken to his sister, but part of him did not want them to be there, he was afraid of Peter and did not know what he intended to do. Alfie sensed that Sofie could be in danger.

"I think you are losing Harry, with too much mind control, he is backing away from us, Peter. it is too much." Alfie said. "And I heard that Jilly and Tina, have asked my mother to warn Sofie to stay away from you."

"Have they now, interfering bitches," Peter snarled. "When I get my full power, I will make everybody in this village pays."

"What have they ever done to you?" Alfie asked.

"My family used to be respected in this village and look what we are reduced to. The house is falling down around my mother and grandmother, and we don't have the funds to do the necessary work."

"But Sofie, she is my little sister. Peter, I don't want to put her in danger," Alfie pleaded.

"Don't be a whimp Alfie," Peter said, staring Alfie down. "You will do what needs to be done. DO YOU UNDERSTAND?" Peter said."

"Yes, Peter," Alfie said, his voice sounded dead like a monotone, then in a blink he seemed normal again. "Okay."

"I will summon them," Peter said, "we need them to come."

"What time are we meeting?" Alfie asked. "Do you need me to bring anything, apart from my friend and my sister?"

"Midnight, bring them with you to the Altar Stone at midnight," Peter commanded. "I have everything else that we will need."

"Okay," Alfie mumbled. "I will try."

"You will do more than try," Peter commanded. "YOU WILL BRING THEM BOTH HERE!"

"Yes Peter," Alfie said.

"Say it!"

"I will bring them here."

The first of May evening service started dead on seven. Jim and Father Jack had shared the proceedings between them, and the choir was prepped to sing.

Brenda sat with Molly and Bert, quite a few people from the village had come and even a few folks from the nearby villages had made the journey.

"How lovely, it sounds wonderful," Molly said, "and the candlelight adds to the magic."

The choir had excelled themselves with a collection of hymns and other songs, and the evening was enjoyed by one and all.

"There are refreshments in the hall," Father Jim said at the end of the service. "Please share a crust with us before making your way safely home. Thank you all for coming."

"It has been our pleasure, "the choir leader said.

People went and drank the fruit punch and to eat some dainties, they chatted and gradually they left, many saying see you tomorrow at the May Fair.

Brenda was exhausted, Molly and Tina helped her clear up before they went home.

"Thank you so much. I would never have got through it without you," Brenda said, she was nearly dead on her feel. "I will get an early night, or I won't be fit for anything tomorrow. Go home safely and thank you again."

"No problem," Molly said. "See you in the morning."

The two ladies and Bert drove off home, Bert giving Tina a lift along the way.

"She looks all in," Tina said, "this has been a lot of work to organize."

"Yes," Molly replied, "been burning the candle at both ends from what I hear."

"What do you mean?" Tina asked.

"Well, I am not one to gossip, but she has been seeing rather a lot of Andy Fitts," Molly said.

"Who told you that? Tina asked.

"Jilly told me, she was seeing Andy, if you know what I mean, but he has told her that he is now in a serious relationship and from now on they could just be good friends."

"Well, I'll be," Tina said. "I had not suspected that."

"It does not surprise me," Bert said.

"Why?" Molly said.

"I saw the way he looked at her at the very first meeting," Bert answered.

"Crickey," Molly said. "I missed that."

"You can't perceive everything, my darling," Bert said. "Here you are Tina, safe and home."

"Thank you and good night, "Tina said. "See you all at the village hall tomorrow morning?"

"I will be there from about eight," Molly replied.

"I will pick up Sofie, and we will load up and come along together, is that okay with you?" Tina asked.

"That is fine," Molly said. "I hope you have a good day. I know that Sofie is looking forward to it. Good night, Tina."

"Let's hope for lovely sunny day."

"I am sure everything is going to go splendidly," Tina remarked as she exited the car and tuned to go inside. "What can go wrong?"

When Brenda had tidied up and returned to the vicarage, Jim was sitting at the kitchen table with a glass of whisky.

"What one?" he asked as Benda entered, indicating the bottle, that sat on the table, next to a pile of papers and receipts.

"No thank you. I think I will have a hot chocolate and go to bed. I am exhausted, and If I don't get a good night's sleep, I will be useless tomorrow."

"Good idea, I think I will do the same," Jim said, "but I just need to unwind a bit first. I will take Terry out to do his business before I come up."

"Good idea, he has been cooped up here for hours, poor boy."

Terry gave a couple of short barks to agree and looked longingly at his lead on the kitchen door.

"See what I mean," she said.

Brenda then made herself a hot chocolate, and with a pat on the head for Terry and a good night to Jim she when up to bed. It was just after ten thirty. Brenda read for half an hour or so, then she put out the light and fell fast asleep.

Brenda did not hear her husband come up to his room, and she did not hear him leave the house over an hour later.

Chapter forty-one

It was a few minutes before twelve, and Peter was waiting by the Altar Stone. He had brought with him all that was needed, the salt and the candles, some herbs, a wad of money, a bottle of whisky and tucked in his belt a large ceremonial knife.

"Where are they?" he muttered to himself. Then he heard voices, and Harry, Sofie and Alfie appeared out of the dark, from under the trees, Alfie was holding a torch.

"At last," he said impatiently. "Let us begin."

"What are we doing here?" Sofie said, looking around." Alfie said there was going to be a party. Is it only us four?"

Harry looked on, but he looked confused as if he did not know why he was there.

"We are here Peter," he said in a dull lackluster voice.

"We are just going to have a bit of fun," Peter said. "Do some harmless magic."

Sofie looked at Alfie in shock. "What?"

"It is okay Sofie," Alfie said, "we have done it before. It's just a harmless ceremony."

"Harry moved forward. He was holding Sofie's hand.

"What do we need to do?" he asked he also sounded weary and unenthusiastic.

"As you are told," Peter retorted, re-imposing his will on Harry.

Peter then made a circle with the salt and put the candles on the four corners using the compass.

"You stand there Sofie, opposite me," he said pleasantly, "and Harry and Alfie either side."

The boys moved into position and Sofie reluctantly followed them on to the Altar stone. "I don't like this," she said.

"Shut up and get into place," Peter snapped, unsettling the girl even more.

"Harry," she said. "I don't like this. I want to go home."

But Harry and Alfie were not listening, they seemed to be acting like robots, and did not answer her, or even look in her direction.

Sofie stood in position, she was terrified. Peter started the ritual, calling to the four elements, before beseeching the Goddess.

"Goddess, we implore you, make us wealthy beyond belief, we bring you our sacrifice," Peter recited, his arms thrown wide. "We offer you our devotion, great lady, our will be done."

It suddenly went very cold, and they all shivered, and a bright light materialized in the middle of the stone circle.

"I answer your summons," the voice said coolly. "What is your sacrifice?"

Peter started to move towards Sofie, but she backed away, and as she stumbled backwards, she knocked over one of the candles and then screamed with fear as she tumbled off the edge of the stone.

Harry suddenly came to his senses. "What are we doing?" he yelled.

The ghostly presence in the middle of the stone disappeared with a pop. There was an unearthly screech, as the witch howled her anger at being thwarted.

"What have you done you stupid bitch," Peter yelled at Sofie, "you have spoilt everything."

Harry jumped off the stone and pulled Sofie up from the ground.

She was dazed and terrified and looked at Harry in bewilderment.

"We must get out of here," he yelled. "Sofie, can you run?"

"I think so," she replied.

Harry and Sofie took off into the trees, and Alfie started to go after them followed by Peter. Sofie was limping badly, but they still managed to get away through the trees and onto the village green.

 "STOP," Peter yelled to Alfie. "We cannot catch them or force Harry to return. Leave it be."

Despite Sofie having hurt herself, the couple were fast, and were well away before the boys could hope to catch them.

Alfie stood panting and Peter turned furiously towards him.

"They have ruined everything," Peter said. The two boys slowly walked back towards the altar stone, to collect their things, but as they approached, they saw the figure of the witch re-form. She was waiting for them and she was very angry.

"You stupid boys, you have ruined things once again. I will not be deprived of my sacrifice." She was enraged.

She raised her arms and blasted them, and they both fell

unconscious onto the grass by the stone. She laughed with maniacal fierceness and began to call for someone to come to her.

"COME TO ME NOW. I have primed you with your obsession, your hunger and your desire, and now is the time to become what you want to be," she shrieked loudly into the night.

Peter and Alfie slowly came to and watched in awe as the spectre of the witch Maud Park Longland did her spell.

Chapter forty-two

When Brenda had gone up to bed, Jim was still buzzing from the success of the evening service and reception, but also from the joy earlier in the day on receiving his fabulous dress. Jim tidied away the papers into the box Brenda had supplied and put it aside.

Terry was acting restless and he went over to the back door and barked while looking around at Jim.

"What do you want Terry?" Jim said, "Do you want to go out?"

The dog was behaving oddly, Jim opened the back door and Terry shot out.

"Come back you mutt, but Terry was standing by the gate barking loudly. "What is wrong with you?" Jim grabbed his collar and hauled him back into the kitchen. "Be quiet Terry. Have a doggie treat, you will wake up the entire village."

The dog stopped barking and picked up his treat and retreated to his basket, but he continued to give Jim a very peculiar look.

Jim sat down to finish his whisky, and again he thought about his new dress.

'It is more beautiful than I could have imagined. It will not hurt to try it on again,' he thought. He ascended to his bedroom he took out the pink stripped box from the bottom of his wardrobe. He opened it and stood rubbing his hand gently over the silky fabric.

"So lovely," he said.

Quickly he slipped off his priestly garb and put on the dress.

"It is so pretty," he said. "I cannot wait for Jeremy's party to show it off," Jim said to himself. "Now what colour eyeshadow would go best with the lilac?"

Jim pulled out his secret hoard of lipsticks and powders and started to experiment with different colours. "The fuchsia lipstick is perfect," he said as he applied it to his lips "And now the wig.

"Hallo Jackeline," Jim said, then he put on the shoes. "Perfect."

It was now just past midnight and Jim stood in front of the mirror admiring himself. "I suppose I had better take it all off and get some sleep," he said, then suddenly he felt the compulsion to stay as he was. A voice was calling him, it was like when he had been in the clearing after the bees had descended on the cricket match.

Jim could not stop himself; he went downstairs and left the house, he did not find it easy to walk on the grass in the high heeled shoes, but he managed and then he found himself on the common heading for the clearing.

"She is coming," Maud Longland said. "Are you ready?"

Chapter forty-three

Harry and Sofie had made their way home after their scare at the Altar Stone. But Sofie was shaking with fear.

"Are you oaky? Harry asked. "You took a nasty fall back here."

"I was really scared Harry. What do they think they are doing?"

"You are shivering, here put on my jacket," Harry said, taking off his jacket and putting around Sofie's shoulders.

Sofie stumbled and Harry reached out to steady her. "You have hurt yourself," he said. "Is it your leg?"

"My right leg folded under me when I fell, and my knee hurts."

"I will see you home safely, lean on me it's not far now," Harry said taking Sofie's arm and supporting her along the street.

When they reached the Travas house, Sofie stopped, and turned towards Harry. Then she burst into tears.

"Should we tell someone what was going on?" she asked trying to control her anxiety, but she was still shaking with fear.

"We don't really know what was going on," Harry said, already his memory of the night's events had already started to fade. "What did happen?"

"I don't actually know. I think maybe that Peter and my brother were just playing a silly game, trying to scare us," Sofie said. "I am so tired. I just want to go to bed. Thank you for seeing me home Harry."

"I couldn't have you wandering the street alone after midnight, now could I, Sofie?" he said taking her hand.

"No, Harry you are so sweet," Sofie said. "Thankyou. Then and she leaned forward and kissed him on the lips. Harry returned her kiss and put his arms around her, but she pulled away.

"Not now Harry. Its late I need to go to bed," she admonished him.

It was then that they were both hit by an atmospheric wave, that disturbed the air. It nearly knocked them off their feet.

"What was that," Sofie asked. "Bloody hell."

"I have no idea, but I don't think it is good," Harry answered.

"It has been a strange night," Sofie said, as she rummaged in her bag for the front door keys.

"See you tomorrow or later today, the May Fair," Harry said.

"I am going to be on a stall with Tina, but I will look out for you. Maybe we can get an ice-cream together or something." She handed him back his jacket.

"Yes Sofie, we will do that," Harry said. "Goodnight."

"Get home safe," Sofie said, and she watched as Harry strolled off down the road back towards the center of the village, on the corner he turned and waved.

"Be safe," Sofie whispered to herself, then she quickly went inside and locked the door behind her.

Jim walked across the village green towards the group of trees at its center. He was not really aware of what he was doing. He just knew that he had to go to the Altar Stone, and that the Goddess was calling him.

"Come to me Jaqueline," she said, "how beautiful you look."

Peter was more alert now, and he realized that the witch was supplying them with a sacrifice, some woman in a wonderful floaty dress, was approaching, and he was ready.

"Go onto the Altar Stone Alfie, now, and re-light the candles."

Alfie moved slowly, but he followed Peter's orders.

Jim/Jaqueline stood looking stunned, until Peter took her hand and led her up onto the Altar Stone.

"DO IT," The witch cried, "do it now."

Peter soon realized what he needed to do, and he held on to Jaqueline's arm and turned her towards the witch.

"By the powers that be, I dedicate this life to my goddess, may she protect us and make us rich beyond our dreams."

Then he took out the knife and slit Jim's throat. Blood spurted out, splashing in a long streak across the Altar Stone, Jim fell limply to the ground dead, as he fell his wig fell off onto the stone shelf and rolled over onto the earth besides the altar stone. The witch laughed hysterically.

"Now you have done it," she cackled. "Peter Frost, your dye is cast. Did you think you could master me? Revenge will be mine"

Then in a flash she disappeared, and Alfie fainted.

Peter was shocked, he did not feel elation, he felt fear, for the first time in his life, he felt really afraid. He fell to his knees and his bladder released, and he felt the warm urine running down his legs. Peter was petrified, and badly shaken.

"What the hell," he said and went over to Alfie where he lay unconscious on the stone. "Wake up, Alfie wake up," Peter said. "She has gone."

Slowly Alfie came to his senses. "What happened," Alfie said, and then he saw the body. "What have we done."

"Let's get out of here," Peter said, gathering up his candles and other paraphernalia.

"What about the body?" Alfie said. "Who is she?"

"I do not know, leave it here, make sure not to leave anything that could identify us."

"Peter was shivering and afraid but continued stuffing things into a carrier bag, "Ready?" then he started walking away and all Alfie could do was follow.

Simultaneously, at twelve-seventeen, all over the village people woke up. Many of the people were jolted awake, while others gently came to, but then rolled over and back into sleep.

A mile away at the Longland house, Anne awoke in the night screaming. Jilly heard her and ran to her room, where Anne was rolling back and forwards, screaming and hugging herself, and then suddenly she lay still."

"Anne, are you alright?" Jilly asked.

Anne seemed not to hear Jilly, but then she turned to her with a blank expression on her face.

"I had a terrible dream, but I know now what I have to do. It is clear, at last. Tomorrow I will be ready," she said to herself, and promptly went back to sleep.

Alana was also jolted out of her sleep, and she knew that something momentous had happened, it was a little while before she slept again. The disturbance in the ether worried her and she knew something momentous was occurring and it could not be good.

Alana did not go back to sleep she lay in her bed pondering about everything that was happening.

"I must phone the Queen in the morning. The start of the May Fair is planned for an eleven o'clock start, with the grand opening planned for twelve noon.' she thought. 'I hope she can come a bit earlier, so we can talk.'

Alana closed her eyes and remembered the marvelous meal and kissing Jilly. I wonder if she is awake?' she thought. 'Jilly, I did not see this coming, I think I love you.'

Alana smiled to herself and turned over but it was a long time before she went back to sleep.

Brenda awoke when she heard Terry barking and went down the kitchen and tried to calm him.

"What's going on Terry? Do you want to go outside?" Brenda went to open the back door and realized that it was not locked in fact it was not even closed properly?

It was still very dark outside and there was a chill in the early morning air. Brenda looked out across the common, the trees on its edge always seemed to stand out as darker that the rest of the area. Brenda shivered and rubbed her arms. Terry was suddenly besides her. He rested against her legs, looked up at her and gave a little whine and then a short sharp bark.

"You alright boy?" Brenda asked. "Something got you spooked?"

He gave another couple of low barks and leaned even closer so her legs. "Let go back in, shall we?"

They returned to the warmth of the kitchen, Brenda closing and bolting the door behind them. Terry retreated to his basket, where he curled himself up and prepared to sleep. Brenda patted his head and turned out the light and went back up to bed.

'Jim must have let Terry out to pee, and not closed the door properly afterwards.' Brenda thought. 'I will have words with him tomorrow.'

Chapter forty-four

May the second, 1959, the May Fair

The sun rose over a picture-perfect English spring day, on May the second. An ideal day for the Little Barnstead May Fair. People all over the village were rising early and getting things ready to make it a wonderful day, one that they would never forget.

Brenda got up just after seven, feeling revitalized and ready for anything after having had a good night sleep.

"Are you up?" she called through her husband's bedroom door. "I am going over to the hall to start getting some things ready."

There was no answer.

'He probably had a bit too much to drink and is sleeping it off,' she thought.

"I will wake him up later," she said as she gave Terry his breakfast and a fresh bowl of water and some food and then let him out to do his business in the garden.

"Sorry to ignore you Terry, we will go for W A L K later, okay?" Terry gave a couple of barks and a look of reproach before he retreated to his basket.

The bottle of whisky and empty glass was still sitting on the kitchen table alongside some biscuit crumbs.

"I wish your dad would clear things up before going to bed," Brenda said.

Terry gave a little bark as if in agreement, before curling up and going back to sleep.

Brenda had not been at the hall long when Molly and Jilly turned up in Bert's car laden with goodies.

"We have enough to feed an army here," Molly said. "Bert, can you feed the children and come back in time for the opening of the Fair at noon?"

"Yes, my pet, see you later," he said.

"Isn't it a beautiful day." Jilly said, as she unloaded trays of food."

"Anne not coming?" Brenda asked.

"I think it is unlikely, she had a restless night and I have left her in bed," Jilly answered. "She did make a cake, I have it here."

"Well, that is a help, poor Anne she seems to be going through a very bad time at the moment," Brenda said.

Molly and Jilly looked sidewise at each other but said nothing more.

"I must go back for my stock. Can you allot me a table?" Jilly said. "See you all in about an hour."

"Yes, I will, when they arrive," Brenda said.

Half an hour later Andy showed up. "The trestle tables have arrived. Where do you want them?" he asked.

"Brenda turned to Molly how many did we decide we needed for the refreshment?"

"Four, I think, maybe six with the cake completion." Molly said. "But the Woman's Institute ladies are bringing their own tables, aren't they?"

"Yes, but we still need some for the hall and a couple more for outside," Brenda added. "And the rest for the traders."

From that moment on, it was complete havoc, as people arrived, and tables were set up. The ladies of Smalltown's Woman's Institute arrived in force and took charge of the cakes and competition tables. Brenda had hardly a moment to think.

"You are my rock," Brenda said to Andy when they managed to get a moment together while making some tea the hall's kitchen.

"You know I am here for you," Andy said. "I will do all I can to help."

"Thank you."

Then Tina and Sofie arrived and Jilly returned, all bearing goods to sell. Andy went about erecting tables in and outside the hall. Alana arrived at just after ten, put out her display of good and asked Jilly to keep an eye on it until she returned with Emelia Rey later.

"You are a treasure," Alana said. "I can't thank you enough. I will make it up to you later."

"I will think of something," Jilly replied with a checky grin.

It was nearly ten thirty when Brenda realized that she had not seen or heard anything from her husband.

"I had better go and find Jim," she said to Molly. "He must have overslept.

When Brenda returned to the kitchen of the Church House

nothing had changed, the bottle of whisky was still on the table.

Brenda automatically tidied it away and then she noticed the dirty mug in the sink.

"Couldn't he have tidied up after himself," she said.

Terry started to bark, and Brenda knew he wanted to go out.

"Just a moment Terry, I want to check if your dad, is upstairs."

Brenda ascended the stair, all was quiet, she knocked on Jim's bedroom door, there was no answer, and then she tried the bathroom, no sign him there either.

"Strange," she said to herself. Brenda walked back to her husband's bedroom and tried the door, it opened, "Jim, are your there?" she asked.

The room was empty if in some disarray, the clothes he had worn the night before left on a chair. Brenda spotted the large pink and white stripped box on the bed, but there was nothing in it except some flimsy tissue paper.

"Stranger and stranger." she said to herself. "He must have had something in it for the fair."

Brenda went back down the stairs and Terry immediately jumped up and barked.

"Okay, I will take you for a short walk, your dad has obviously gone out somewhere."

So, Brenda took Terry out into the road and walked a short way on the village green. Terry relieved himself and seemed much calmer.

"Better now?" she asked. Terry was reluctant to have his walk cut short and barked once to show his displeasure before allowing them to go quietly home.

"Now I must wash and change to get ready to open this May Fair." Brenda said, speaking to Terry. "I think it is going to be quite a day. Where on earth is Jim?"

Chapter forty-five

At Frost House Meggie got up early to take Lady Jane a cup of tea in bed. She had not been well for the last few days and looked weak and very pale.

"I am off to the May Fair with some food, is there anything that you want before I go?"

"No, my dear. I don't know what I would do without you."

"I could get you some toast," Meggie said. "Or a boiled egg?"

"Not just now. I will get up later and make myself something. Is Peter going to the May Fair with you?"

"I am not sure. I have not seen him yet. He was out very late last night."

When Meggie went back down to the kitchen Peter was sitting at the table having a cup of coffee.

"Are you coming to the May Fair?" Meggie asked.

"Yes, I will come over later," he answered, then changes his mind. "No, I will come with you. What time are you going?"

"I am going over about eleven, I have some food to take for the sale tables."

"Okay," Peter replied. "I will give you a hand, let me know when you are leaving."

'I have to act naturally.' he thought to himself. 'Nobody must suspect.'

Peter made himself some breakfast while Meggie was doing last minute preparation for some savory quiches, and they drove over to the May Fair at about eleven fifteen.

Anne had woken up when the atmospheric jolt hit in the early hours. She had gone back to sleep, but she was very restless for the remainder of the night. Jilly had looked in on her again in the morning, about ten.

"I am off now, Anne," Jilly said. "Are you coming over later?"

"Don't know," Anne had said. "I am that tired." And then Anne rolled over and went back to sleep.

"Okay, I may see you later," Jilly said. 'Please yourself,' she thought, 'probably better if she does not come.'

When Anne finally got up and went down to the kitchen, she moved very slowly, and seemed not to be very aware of anything. But then she looked over at the kitchen table and nodded.

"You're here again," she said. "What is the time?"

Anne was shocked to see by the kitchen clock that it was half past one in the afternoon. "I am so hungry," she said, again looking towards the kitchen table.

"Good day to you," she said. "I am so glad so see you. Do you want a cup of tea? I am going to make myself a sandwich."

Anne bustled around boiling water, then she took two mugs from the cupboard and placed them on the table. She poured out two mugs of tea and put one on the table opposite her. "Do you want sugar? I seem to remember that you had a sweet tooth."

Anne was talking to her dead fiancé. She started spooning sugar into the mug of tea, when she reached about eight spoonful's she stopped and looked up.

"You're not really here, are you? You didn't come back to me. I am so alone." Anne put her head on the table and wept, then she lashed out with her right arm and knocked over the mug of tea. "Why am I so alone?" she wailed.

"ANNE," a voice bellowed. "Anne, listen to me, you know what you have to do. Get yourself together NOW."

Anne jumped up in fear. "What?" she said.

"Anne, you know what I require you to do, get what is needed. Get it now."

Anne did not react, it seemed that her body had lost its momentum, and she just sat there in a trance. "What?" she mumbled again, but she did not attempt to get up and move. Once again, her head rested on the kitchen table and she seemed to be sleeping.

The witch continually tried to get her up and moving.

"ANNE," she called repeatedly, and then in desperation she sent a bolt of hard cold energy into Anne's body. Anne jumped as she felt it and screamed. And then Anne was in the witch's power once more.

"You are hurting me, let me be," Anne said crying piteously.

"I will not let you be, get moving," The witches voice ordered. "Get the necessary things together. Anne, you know what needs to be done. Abide by my will. DO IT NOW."

Anne stood up and looked around and then she picked up an ancient straw shopping bag and put some old newspapers into it.

"Fuel, you need fuel and matches," the witch commanded.

Anne turned to the cupboard and took out a bottle of cooking oil and then she added it to the basket.

"What else?" Anne asked, looking around vacantly.

"Matches," the witch shouted. "Get matches."

Anne picked up some matches from the shelf next to the cooker, and held them in her hand, staring at them, before she put them in the basket.

"Go to Frost House, go now," the witches voice said.

Anne picked up her basket and left the kitchen leaving the door wide open. Slowly she headed off towards Frost House, a twenty-minute walk away down the lane. Anne walked in a trance and paused on small bridge over the river that crossed the Frost Estate. She stood absent mindedly gazing down into the water

"Anne, get moving," the witch said, nudging Anne into motion once more.

When Anne reached Frost House and just stood and gazed up at the front of the building.

"Go round to the kitchen, the door is open," the voice ordered.

When Anne entered the kitchen, she stood and looked around. The remains of a breakfast were still sitting on the table and two dirty cups were in the sink. The door to the rest of the house was closed. Suddenly all the doors in the house crashed open, as the witch sent a bolt of energy through the residence.

Lady Jane heard this and thought that Meggie or Peter had returned.

"Meggie is that you?" she called.

Anne did not hear her because she was in a trance and under the witch's spell, and nothing else made any impact on her consciousness.

"Lay the fire," the witch's voice commanded. "DO IT NOW."

Anne put the basket on the floor near the Aga and crumpled up the newspapers then she poured the cooking oil over it.

Anne suddenly stopped and stared around her.

"What am I doing?" she asked. "Where am I?"

The witch re-focused her control over Anne.

"Light the fire," she commanded. "Light it now. I will have my revenge, and I will have it now."

Anne struck the match and dropped it onto the newspapers. It ignited straight away, and flames shot up in the air catching a tea towel that was hanging on the side of the aga.

Anne screamed as the flames quickly traveled across the kitchen floor and out into the hallway. Then the witch released her control on Anne's mind. Anne, now confused and disorientated ran in a panic away from Frost House. Her mind was no longer possessed, but what was left was a confused and emptied void.

Anne was no longer controlled by the witch, but she was not quite sane either, all rational thought seemed to have gone.

She walked down to the riverside and sat, gazing out over the water.

And that is where Jilly found her many hours later.

"Anne," Jilly asked, "Are you okay?"

Anne just gazed up at her sister her face vacant.

"He didn't come back," she said. "But I have my baby."

She was singing an old lullaby and cradled in her lap was a very large spotted toad.

"Oh Anne, my sister, where have you gone?"

Anne looked up at Jilly. "Jilly, my little sister, I do love you." Then her face went blank, and she spoke no more.

Chapter forty-six

When Brenda returned to the village hall, about eleven thirty, after taking Terry for his walk. There was a lot of activity. She had still not seen or heard anything about Jim's whereabouts, and was getting a bit worried as to where he had gotten to. Molly was frantically making teas and serving customers with food, and there were a lot of people milling about.

"You look busy," Brenda said. "Do you need help?"

"It's been non-stop since eleven. I hope we have enough food," Molly said. At that moment Bert arrived with Alfie, Kate, and Brian.

"Kate my darling, please give me a hand for a while until someone else arrives to help. Gladys is coming, but she had to collect something at the shop first."

"Okay mum, but I want to go and see what is happening outside as well."

Sofie had arrived earlier with Tina and they had set up a table with their kitchen items, decorated cushions and other bit and pieces. The table was next to Jilly and her statues and figures, and Alana's goods were next to Jilly's.

"We are going to take another table or two outside and sell the cold drinks from there. Bert, would you get that sorted for me the tables are over there, Andy will help you," Molly said.

"No problem, my darling," Bert said. "Your wish is my command."

"You will get your reward," Molly quipped.

"Promises, promises, that all I get," Bert replied, taking himself off the tackle the trestle tables.

"By the way Brenda, the Women's Institute ladies say we should sell off the cakes after the competition, make if for a good cause of something."

"What a good idea. There is a stand outside for cancer research outside."

"That would work," Molly replied. "Do you want to speak to them?"

"Yes, I will do that now," Brenda said.

Alfie saw Peter and Meggie arrive and went over to meet them.

"Hallo, Mrs Frost," Alfie said. "I hope you are well. Lady Frost not coming?"

"No Alfie, she is not feeling too well and has stayed in bed," Meggie replied, then she noticed Molly.

"Molly looks as if she could do with a hand," Meggie said. "Peter, could you carry these trays of foods over to the hall for me?"

"No problem, Mum," Peter replied." Peter and Alfie took a tray each and took them over to the hall and put them on an empty trestle table.

"Thank you, boys. See you later," Meggie said as she hustled off to help unload things and deposit the new supplies on the food and drinks stall.

"Thank you, Meggie, poor Molly is rushed off her feet," Brenda said, as she followed her into the hall. "And we are going put a second eating point outside. Bert and Andy are just getting it set up."

Brenda went outside and started to look around to see who had arrived and see if there was any sign of Jim, when Andy came rushing up to her.

"Brenda. They are here," he said. "Where is your husband?"

"I don't know, I can't find him," Brenda said.

"Well, you had better come and meet them. They came in a Silver Cloud Rolls Royce," Andy said with an awed expression on his face.

Emelia Rey pulled up outside the Church House and stepped out of the car. Alana, Hermosa, and Kigali followed her like a guard of honor. Brenda rushed forwards to meet them.

"Welcome, welcome to our May Fair. It is so good of you to come and open it for us," she said. "We are ready for you."

"It is my pleasure," Emelia said. "Everything looks very festive."

She looked stunning in a floral summer dress and a straw hat with flowers on the edge, her blond hair loose and shiny hanging over her shoulders. She had pulled out all the stops and gone for the English country rose, come ethereal goddess look.

Accompanied by the beautiful golden Hermosa and the elegant black figure of Kigali, they made quite a spectacle.

There were at least a hundred people milling around and a good third of them were men, who all gasped at the Queen's beauty and poise. But some of the women admired her but envied her obvious fame and good looks.

Harry had arrived just as Emelia Rey and was being swamped by crowds of people who were there to see her to open the fair. He looked around and went to talk to Sofie and him mum on their stall.

They watched as the car pull in.

"Here she comes," Sofie exclaimed.

The group surrounding the car grew as the queen emerged to be greeted by Brenda.

"She is very beautiful," Sofie said, "But, I don't remember seeing any of her films. And her companions are stunning."

"Nor do I. Yes, she is lovely, but not as pretty as you," Harry replied, with a wink. "Do you want an ice cream?" he asked.

"Yes, please," Sofie said. "You charmer."

"Would you like one mum?" Harry asked.

"I would prefer a cup of tea. You go get an ice cream, and then perhaps you would stay with Sofie while I nip to the loo and get some tea and cake for myself," Tina said.

"No problem, "Harry said. He walked over to the ice cream van, on the way he saw Peter and Alfie and nodded in their direction. They waved back, but did not move from their spot, next to the cold drinks table.

The ice cream van was parked on the road near the village green and was doing a great business. Quite a few people were waiting in line, but they had all turned around to watch when Emelia Rey arrived.

Peter and Alfie were standing near the entrance to the hall, when the car pulled up, and they looked impressed.

"What do you think" Peter asked.

"She is gorgeous," Alfie replied. "Definitely fuckable."

"We can have plenty of women like that every day, when we are rich and powerful," Peter said.

"I would not be so sure of that, last night did not go exactly as we hoped," Alfie said, he glanced nervously around that the gathering.

"We will see," Peter muttered quietly. "Stop looking so furtive, we must act normally."

"It's not that easy." Alfie fidgeted. "There's Harry."

"He is cool, don't fret, for god's sake keep it together Alfie."

"I am trying to, but …"

"Keep calm, for heaven's sake," Peter said. "Nobody is going to suspect us. We have to act like normal."

Chapter forty-seven

"One two three," Brenda said into the microphone. "I have always wanted to do that," she laughed. "People of Little Barnstead and surrounds, please give a big Devon welcome to Emelia Ray."

Amid a roar of cheers and clapping, Queen Emelia Rey stepped up to the microphone.

"Hallo my friends, it is so nice to see you all on this glorious day. It is my pleasure to open this Little Barnstead May Fair. Blessings to the Fair and all who sail in her," she said, with a huge smile that won nearly everybody's hearts.

Hermosa and Kigali stood behind her and somehow, they seemed to be able to stop anybody coming too close. The people at the Fair were fascinated by Kigali, many had never seen a black man, up close, except some black American GI's during the war. He was very imposing and handsome in his own way, dressed in a dark emerald green suit and pale lime coloured shirt. Hermosa matched him in a sunny yellow and green dress and matching green shoes. They both looked unworldly against the blandness of the English countryside.

"Would you like a drink and a piece of cake?" Brenda asked.

"That would be lovely," Emelia Rey said, and they walked over to the trestle tables that had now been erected outside the church hall, with drinks and a selection of cakes, sandwiches, and savory items.

Molly was serving, and she almost fainted when the Queen asked what kinds of cakes they had.

"There are sponges and fruit cakes or my own specialty carrot cake." Molly enthused. "There are also flans and salads and lots of other things inside."

"I will have a piece of your carrot cake," Emelia Ray said, indicating to Hermosa to get it for her. "And a cold drink, I think, it is quite hot today. Lemon squash will do."

Andy had put out some chairs up outside the hall and Brenda steered Emelia Rey and her retinue over to them to have their cake and drinks.

"Are you saying in the area long?" Brenda asked.

"I am not sure at the moment," the Queen replied. "This cake is delicious."

"Why, there is Jilly," the Queen exclaimed we must go and see her stall."

Hermosa took the dirty plates and return them to Molly. "Emelia Rey loved your cake," she said with a big smile. "Could you let us have the recipe?"

Molly looked very pleased that the queen had relished eating her own homemade cake.

"Why, yes, of course. I will let Alana have it." Molly could not have been prouder. "She liked my cake," she said to herself.

With Hermosa and Kigali on each side of her. Alana and Brenda in their wake, they progressed across the grass to the area where several people had goods on display and for sale.

"Jilly darling how wonderful to see you," Emelia gushed and kissed her on the cheek. Then she picked up one of the ornamental door number plaques that Jilly had made and passed it to Hermosa. "Can you do these to order?" she asked.

"Yes," Jilly replied. "I can make them any size, a number or with a picture."

"We must order one for the villa in Italy," Emelia Rey said. "Can you do something with grapes or sunflowers?"

"Yes, I can let you have a sketch, for your approval."

"Looking after Alana's goods, are you? That's kind."

Then she noticed Tina's table, which was next door to Alana's.

"And what are these gorgeous cushions?" she asked. "Oh, and little herb bags, how adorable."

Picking one up and putting it to her nose she exclaimed. "Lavender and a bit of rosemary and thyme and is that basil? I love the smell of basil. You make these?" she asked. "Look at the embroidery Hermosa, it is so delicate."

"Basil, good at aiding sleep," Tina said. "My assistant Sofie here, does the finishing touches and embroidery."

Sofie had embroidered little sprigs of lavender on the edges of the bags and some of the cushions and other items.

"They are absolutely gorgeous," Amelia Rey said, selecting several items and putting them to one side.

"I feel another buying spree coming on," Hermosa whispered to Kigali. He nodded and they shared a smile behind the Queens back.

Emelia Rey wandered around the fair, somehow managing to keep people at a distance. Hermosa and Kigali had their arms full of purchases in no time. Emelia stopped to talk to the man doing basket work, but he was so nervous he could hardly speak."

"What are these?" Emelia asked, holding up one of his skillfully woven trugs.

"They are trugs, people use them when picking vegetables or flowers in the garden." Brenda said.

"How adorable," Emelia said, picking up two and passing them to Hermosa to pay. "And you have a besum. Can I buy that?"

"You can," the trader replied. "But I only have the one, can you collect it later, so that I can keep it on display?"

"No problem," Emelia said turning to Hermana. "Will you remember that?"

"Yes, your majesty," Herman replied. "I will see to it."

"Will you excuse me, Emelia? I have to go see what is happening in the hall," Brenda said.

"Of course, Brenda you go. I am well looked after, come Alana show me your wares, and I must decide which of Jilly's figures to commission for my Chelsea Garden."

Brenda went off to speak to Molly. "It's going very well," she said. "Have you seen Jim?"

"No," Molly answered. "Not a sight of him. Is something wrong?"

"I have not seen him today, where has he got to?" Brenda was now more than a little concerned.

"The cake competition was now being judged and one of the ladies from the Woman Institute approached Brenda.

"Do you think that Emelia Rey would present the winner with her prize?" The lady from the Woman's Institute asked.

"I don't know, I will ask her," Brenda replied.

"I would be delighted," Emelia said, when she was asked.

The May Fair had been going quite a few hours and now the cakes were being sold off, everybody seemed to be having a great time.

"What a wonderful day," Meggie said. "And we are so lucky with the weather."

At that moment a man carrying a distraught little boy came running up from the far end of village green, in a state of panic.

"There is a body on the Altar Stone, a woman has been killed," the man cried.

Chapter forty-eight

As the news gradually spread through the crowds, there was a low rumble and then outrage, panic and confusion.

Harry and Sofie were eating their ice creams when they heard the news and they both suddenly went very pale and looked over at Peter and Alfie. Luckily Peter did not notice them because when Peter and Alfie heard the news Alfie started shaking and his face went ashen, he looked as if he was going to faint.

"Hold it together, for God's sake," Peter muttered. "We left nothing there to lead to us."

"But, Harry and Sofie, they know we were there?"

"I don't think that they will remember much. I did that whammy on them remember," Peter said.

Alfie still looked decidedly frantic and ready to run.

"Let's go and get a drink from your mum, and ask what is going on," Peter said. "Act normally."

They walked over to the refreshment table where a few people were talking nervously.

"Hi Mum, what is going on?" Alfie asked, trying to sound casual.

"They have found a woman's body on the Old Altar Stone. She has been stabbed," Molly said. "I don't know any more than that, the police have been called."

"Crickey," Peter exclaimed. "What's this place coming to."

At the same time Jilly, Alana and Emelia Rey were huddled together with Emelia's assistants outside the hall by Alana's stall.

"How come I didn't feel this happening?" Emelia asked in confusion, looking around at her companions. Hermosa and Kigali both shook their heads. "I felt nothing Majesty," Hermosa said.

"Nor I," Kigali added.

"I told you this morning, there was a shudder in the atmosphere last night, it woke me up," Alana said. "You were probably too far away to feel it."

Jilly was looking very agitated. "I think I did, very early this morning there was like a disturbance in the air. I woke up, it was about twenty past twelve, Jilly said. "I checked on Anne and she was very distressed, I tried to settle her and then I went back to bed."

"Hold my hands," Emelia said. They stood in a huddle and Emelia sent out a wave of enquiry, she also sent waves of empathy to calm the crowd who were meandering around and becoming very restless.

"It is muddle, but the person responsible is here, very near to us."

They broke away from each other and looked around at the throng of people milling around.

"I can't get a handle on it," Emelia said. "I will cast a locator spell."

Emelia stood very still and concentrated on the crowds of people milling around her.

"There is very strong presence here and it is blocking me."

The Queen was turning pale with the effort of trying to find the culprit. "There is something evil here and I can't get a hold on it. I think we had better leave. Let's go back to your shop Alana and try again."

"I must see to my goods," Alana said. "I can't leave Jilly to deal with it all. Go to my flat."

"Okay, we will catch up with you both later," Emelia Rey said. "Come Hermosa, Kigali, we need to go. Now."

"I will see you later," Alana said. "At the flat?"

"Yes. Give Kigali the key," Emelia Rey said, her voice trembled.

"Okay." Alana and Jilly hurried off to pack up their sales tables.

The Queen and her assistants departed in the Rolls Royce to go to the flat above Pandoras Box to wait for Alana. They all appeared very shaken.

"The presence is very strong. I can feel it. but I can't locate it," Emelia said despairingly. "Who is it?" she paused, "It is so strong."

"I think it is the witch," Hermosa said. "And she is not finished yet."

Chapter forty-nine

Brenda was standing outside the village hall. She looked shocked, her face had gone pale as chalk.

"Are you okay?" Andy asked. "I am going to go to the Altar Stone to stop anybody touching anything, the police will want to see it as is," Andy said. He took Brenda's hand. "Are you going to be, okay?"

She nodded.

"I will stay with her," Meggie said, "come and have cup of tea Brenda."

Meggie led Brenda away to the back of the hall.

"I'll come too," Mr Potts said to Andy. "My wife has gone home."

"Shall I come with you?" Bert asked.

But just then Molly came in from outside and joined them.

"Molly, I think we should pack things up," Andy said. "The May Fair is ended; people are starting to leave. I am going out to the murder sight to keep it clear for the police"

"Yes, that's a good idea," she replied, "I will find the kids and get Alfie to take them back to the house."

"Okay, I will see you later Darling," Bert said. "What a thing to happen …"

"I know Bert. I can't believe it." Molly was in tears. "Come home as soon as you can."

"Hold it together for the kids, Molly …" Bert put his arm around

Molly's shoulders and kissed her cheek. "I will be home as soon as I can."

Brenda felt ghastly, but after having a strong cup of tea she started to help people pack things away and clear up.

"We must clear up," she muttered. "What a terrible ending, to what seemed such a perfect day," Brenda muttered to Meggie.

The ladies from the Women's Institute were efficient as ever, and soon had their tables empty and the leftovers packed up.

Brenda thanked them and went outside to see what needed doing. Almost all the traders had packed up and gone, the few remaining people were just hanging around. Molly having dispatched her children off home had cleared her tables and was endeavoring to take down the trestles.

"Leave them," Brenda said, "Andy will sort it out."

"Tina approached Molly.

"Sofie is very upset. I will give her a lift home, after we have returned our goods to the shop. Is that okay with you Molly? Luckily there is not much left to pack." Tina said quietly to Molly. "I will not leave her there alone and I can stay with your children until you or Bert get home."

"Thank you. That is good of you Tina," Molly said. "I will just finish up here and then I will be off as well. But I want to make sure that Brenda is okay first."

When Alfie was asked to take his brother and sister home, Peter stayed and watched the May Fair being dismantled. But when the police arrived, he decided to make a move and head home.

"Mum, I am going to go back now," he told Meggie. "See you later."

"Okay Peter. Don't worry about tea, I will have some food to bring home. Please check on your grandmother," she said, and she smiled at her son. "What a day?"

"Yes Mum," Peter said. "I will see you at home when you have finished here."

"Yes, see you later love," Meggie said. "Please go straight home."

"I will mum, don't you worry."

"Where is the body?" the detective said. Addressing nobody in particular. Luckily Andy was were just returning from the murder scene, he looked grim.

"I will show you," Andy told the policeman. "Mr Potts is still there making sure that nobody touches anything." Andy was looking around for Brenda and saw her standing outside the village hall.

Andy led the policemen off over the common to the murder location, as they approached the scene Mr Potts emerged from the stand of trees and waved.

"Andy," he said grabbing his arm and whispering something in his ear.

"What, oh my god," Andy said, and then he turned to return to the Church Hall.

"We will need to speak to you. What is your name?" the police officer asked.

"I am Andy Fitts; I live just across the way from the church."

"I will see you later," The policeman said. "Where will you be?"

"I will be in the hall or in the church house." Andy replied.

As Andy walked back across the green another police van arrived with the forensic team and he pointed them off toward the Altar Stone, then he returned to look for Brenda. Finding her standing gathering up chairs outside the church hall.

"Brenda," Andy said, and he took her arm and guided her into the hall. There were very few people left there now, Molly and Meggie had everything under control.

"Can you stack the trestle tables please Andy? They are a bit much for us," Molly asked.

"No problem. I will stack them in the hall and leave a message for the company to collect them," he said. "Just leave it to me."

He led Brenda to a chair at the back of the hall and then went and stacked up the tables and made sure that there were none left outside.

Molly and Meggie approached Brenda and asked if she was okay, then they left.

"Call me if you need anything," Molly said. "Jilly has gone home to check on Anne."

"I don't think you should be on your own, where is your husband anyway? I have not seen him all day?" Meggie asked.

"I don't know," Brenda said. "I will be fine Andy will stay with me."

The ladies left just as Andy was returning with the last stray tables from outside.

"Will you stay with her? she is very upset," Molly asked.

"I will. Thank you for all your help today. I can't believe what is happening." Andy shrugged. "Thank you, ladies."

Brenda joined Molly and Meggie before they left, Bert had just rejoined them.

"Thank you," Brenda said. "Thank you so much."

When everybody had gone. Andy shut the hall door and returned to Brenda, he opened his arms and she walked into them.

"Oh Brenda," he said.

"Was it awful?" she asked.

"You should go home," he said and led her through to the back kitchen and over to her own house.

"Will the police want to speak to me?" she asked.

"Yes, I expect they will. But I told them we would be in the hall or in the church house."

Brenda entered her kitchen and Terry ran up to her and rested his head against her legs, then he sniffed at Andy and went back to his basket where he sat, his eyes not leaving Brenda for a moment.

"I will make some coffee," she said. "Do you want some?"

"Come and sit down," he requested. "I will make you a drink."

He made two mugs of strong coffee and added a large spoonful of sugar. Then he sat down next to Brenda and took her hand.

"Brenda?" he said.

"What is it?" she demanded.

"It was Jim," he said.

"I know," she replied. "I think I knew. I have not seen him since last night." Brenda sighed, "and, he was dressed as a woman?"

"Yes, and his throat was cut, he was lying on the Altar Stone."

"Oh my god." Brenda choked on her coffee and tears came to her eyes.

Andy stood and pulled Brenda into his arms.

"Did you know? Did you know that Jim was a cross dresser?" Andy asked. "You should have told me."

"I wanted to, Andy. But it is not easy. I could not just say my husband is a transvestite."

"You could tell me anything Brenda. I love you."

"Andy, this is so terrible. Does everybody know?" she asked.

"I doubt that the police will broadcast it straight away, but they will find out, there will have to be an investigation. It looks as if he was ritually murdered," Andy said, caressing Brenda's back.

"They are going to want to talk with me," Brenda said.

And at that moment there was a knock on the front door.

Chapter fifty

As Peter walked back towards Frost house, his mind was going over the murder scene. 'I am sure we left no clues,' he thought. 'I threw the knife in the river; they won't find that.'

He was crossing the old East field, as a shortcut to the house, when suddenly he nearly tripped over something that was protruding from the grass.

'What the hell,' he thought, there was something sharp poking out. 'What is this.' Peter grabbed the object and pulled it out of the earth, it was a human leg bone. He dropped the bone quickly and a chill went down his spine. "Bloody hell," he exclaimed.

As he carried on towards his home, he smelt the smoke, and he started to run, and then he saw the flames.

'Frost House is burning,' he thought. 'Grandmother is inside.'

Peter came to a halt in front of the house, flames were evident in upper windows. Peter went to the front door and opened it. A blast of heat nearly pushed him backwards.

The hall was clear of fire, but full of smoke. Peter cautiously entered and grabbed an old raincoat, and headscarf of his mother's, that was hanging in the hallway. He tied the scarf over his mouth and nose. When he reached the main staircase, he could see that flames were blocking it.

"The back stairway," he said. "The servant's stair, that should be clear." He pulled the old coat over his head and shoulders and cautiously walked along the hall to the back of the house.

As Peter passed the kitchen, he saw that it had been gutted, it was still very hot and he could even feel the heat through his shoes, but he could easily reach the old servant stone stairway.

The door was stiff, but he managed to open it. There was a lot of smoke but no fire. People did not bother to put carpet in areas just used by servants, so the stone stairway had nothing in it that was flammable.

'This might do,' Peter thought. 'If I can get past the first floor.'

Peter climbed the stairway and reached the upper floor, he had great difficulty opening the door on to the second-floor landing, then he remembered. 'There is an old cupboard in front of the door, this stair is no longer used.'

It took a bit of effort, to shunt the cupboard forward, but Peter finally managed to open the door enough for him to slip through.

There was a lot of smoke and he could see that some of the rooms were on fire, then he heard a muffled scream.

"Oh my god, grandma is trapped in her bedroom," he muttered, his voice muffled by the smoke. "Granny are you there," he croaked the heat burning his throat, there was no reply.

He could see that the hallway along the corridor was engulfed in flame, but he tried to make some progress down the hallway. "Grandma are you there?" Peter tried to shout again, but his voice was gone, smoke and heat had filled his mouth and were searing his throat.

'She is gone,' he thought. 'I have to get out of here before it all goes up.' Flames were leaping along the corridor now and because of the draft from the old stair way had caught the cupboard and its surrounding area. 'I cannot return that way,' he thought. 'God help me I am trapped.'

His only option was the main staircase. 'It's a bit clearer now, but decidedly hot and smoky,' he thought as he made his way through the gloom towards the central stairway. He could hardly see in the fug and the heat was terrible, burning his throat and stinging his eyes. A chandelier had come loose and dropped on the landing in front of the stairs, in the gloom Peter did not see it and he fell. Falling awkwardly to the landing halfway between the first two floors, one leg painfully trapped beneath the other.

'My chest hurts, and I think I have broken my leg,' he thought in panic. "There is no way out," he said, in a choked whisper.

"You are right," the voice said. "There is no way out for you."

"Who? Who are you?" Peter tried to say, but his throat was closing, and he was in great pain as he had also broken several ribs, it was impossible for him to move. The flames were getting nearer, the heat was terrible. Peter could see a shimmering light as the form of a young women took shape.

"What?" he tried to say but all that came out was a muffled groan.

"I am Maud Park Longland, your forebears killed my mother and then had me burned at the stake. I have come to take my revenge. I have not forgotten. I have many grievances against your family."

Peter heard this but he was quickly losing awareness of his surroundings as the fire consumed his body.

"What?" he croaked, "No, he screamed but his voice was gone ...." And then he slipped away, his consciousness leaving just his body to be consumed by the flames.

"Now you will feel what it is like to burn to death," she guffawed at his pain, when the last spark of life left him, she departed, screeching with glee and his demise.

"I can be at peace now," she said. "There are no men left of the Frost blood line. My work is done."

Her form blinked out and Maud Park Longlands's spirit vanished from this world forever.

Chapter fifty-one

When the police knocked on her front door Brenda looked up at Andy, her face set in stoic acceptance.

"You go and let them in," she said. "Please."

Andy nodded and went to let in the police. There were three of them two men and a young woman, they looked very disturbed by what they had seen. Andy led them through to the kitchen where Brenda was sitting at the kitchen table. Terry started to bark when the three strangers entered the kitchen, but Andy put his hand on Terry's head and he instantly calmed down and went to his basket. But the dog kept his eyes on Brenda and the other occupants of the room. The policeman did not miss Andy's familiarity, in calming the dog, and wrote something in his notebook.

"I am Detective Sergeant Brownload. I believe I am speaking to Mrs Brenda Noakes, is that right?" the most senior policeman asked.

"Yes, I am Mrs Noakes," Brenda replied.

"I am sorry, but we have some bad news for you," the inspector said.

"I know, it is about my husband."

Brenda was nervous but she knew she had to answer their questions.

"Yes, he is dead, we think it is some sort of ritual. He was found stabbed this afternoon on the Altar Stone. You know the one just off the village green? Our forensics people think he died sometime during the night. We are not sure exactly what time yet, but at least twelve or more hours ago. We will know more when we get him back to the coroner's office." He paused. "They will give us a report in due course," he said. "Can we ask you a few questions?"

"Yes," Brenda replied. "I want to help."

"When did you last see your husband?"

"Friday night," she replied.

"At what time?"

"I think it was about half passed ten."

"Did you know where he had gone?"

"No," Brenda said, her voice going high with tension. "We have separate bedrooms, so I did not know that he had gone out."

Brenda swallowed and then looked up at the Detective.

"I am sorry Mrs Noakes, but we need to know as much as possible about what happened prior to the murder," Detective Brownload said. "So, you did not see or hear anything from your husband after ten thirty on Friday night?"

"That is correct. I looked for him Saturday morning, and a few times during the day. It was hectic all day, because of the May Fair, and nobody had seen anything of him," Brenda said nearly choking over her words.

"So, as far as you know he was at home when," He consulted his notebook. "10.30 Friday night when you last saw him?"

"Yes, when I went to bed, he was sitting at our kitchen table. We had held a service and musical evening in the church, and he was still excited at how well it had gone."

"I see. We believe that he was taken… He either went willingly or by force, to the Altar Stone, and that is where he was killed," the detective said.

"I see," Brenda answered, but she was wondering when he would get around to the cross-dressing aspect of the case.

"Did you husband have any enemies, that you know of?" the detective asked.

"I don't think so," she replied. "He was generally well liked. We have not lived here very long, so we are, I mean we were, still getting to know people." Brenda sobbed and her hand went to her mouth, but then she brought herself back under control. "I'm sorry," she said. Brenda wiped her eyes on a tea towel, folded it and put it on the table in front of her, and looked up at the detective.

"It's okay, I know that this is difficult for you, but I have to ask." The police officer hesitated. "Did you know? I mean were you aware that your husband dressed up in female clothes?" the officer asked.

A younger constable sniggered, and the inspector gave him a censuring look.

"I did know," Brenda said. "He was a transvestite."

"I see," the inspector said. He did not seem able to continue this line of questioning. "I will have more questions, in due course. And I will need you to come and identify the body. Can you do that in the morning?"

"Yes, I will do that," Brenda replied. "Please tell me the address."

"I have a card with the address and the case number," the detective said, putting a piece of paper on the table in front of Brenda.

"Thank you, Detective Brownload. I will help anyway I can," Brenda said.

"Do you have someone who can stay with you? Constable Jill Betts could stay with you if you want her to?" he said indicating the female police officer.

"I am fine. Andy will stay with me," Brenda said, looking up at Andy for his assent.

"Off course I will. I only live across the road. So that will be no problem," Andy said all in a rush. "Of course, I will stay."

"Okay, that will be all for now," the man moved to go but then he turned again towards Brenda." Just one more thing, do you know any of your husband's transvestite friends?" he asked.

"No, I don't," Brenda replied. "I never did."

"I see, can we search his room?" The detective asked. "There may be something there to help us."

"Of course," Brenda said. "It's at the top of the stairs on the left."

"Thank you Mrs Noakes."

"His diary and address book are in the front room next to the telephone. But I will need the address book to let people know about the death." Brenda choked back a tear and looked down at her hands. "Oh my God, I have to tell my father."

"That is fine we will copy the information and return the book to you tomorrow."

"Thank you, Detective," Brenda said, she could no longer hold back the tears and was no crying into the old tea towel.

"Mr Fitts, could we speak to you?" The detective asked and indicating by his head movement that he meant away from Brenda. Andy looked down at Brenda and she nodded her head.

"Of course," Andy replied.

The two male police officers accompanied Andy into the hall way, and the female office remained with Brenda.

"Do you know the family well?" Detective Sergeant Brownload asked.

"Not that well, they only moved here this year but ... Brenda... Mrs Noakes and I have become close."

"I see, and you will stay with her."

"Yes, do you think I should call the doctor? He may prescribe her a sedative or something?"

"I think that would be a good idea We will have a look at Mr Noakes room and then we will be off."

After twenty minutes the Detective Sergeant Brownload returned to the kitchen where he said good bye and reminded Brenda to go and identify the body the following morning.

Constable Jill Betts had been sitting with Brenda, and she now stood up to leave.

"You have our phone number Mrs Noakes, if you need to talk,

please do call me or Detective Sergeant Brownload."

"I will. I will be okay," Brenda said, "Andy will stay with me."

"If you are sure Brenda," the police woman asked.

"Yes, I am sure. I will come in to the station in the morning."

When the front door closed Andy walked back into the kitchen and he opened his arms and Brenda stepped into them.

"My poor darling, I knew that there was something … you should have told me."

"I wanted too, but did not know how," Brenda whispered. "Please just hold me, Andy."

Andy enfolded Brenda in his arms and rested his cheek next to hers. His hands gently rubbing her back.

"I want to hold you and be there for you forever Brenda, you do know that don't you. We will get through this. I promise."

"Yes, Andy I believe we will."

Brenda stepped away from Andy and sat down at the table and picked up her cup of coffee.

Terry who had been watching all these comings and goings, walked over to Brenda and put his head in her lap.

Chapter fifty-two

It was Sunday morning when the news of the deaths reached
Molly and her family. They had seen the fire, but there was so
much confusion that they could not get near the main house or get
any information from the fire bigrade and police that were on the
scene. So, they all went to bed before hearing of the death of Peter
and Lady Jane or that it was Father Jim that had been murdered.

"Molly, have your heard?" Brenda had said into the phone.

"What?" Molly replied.

"My Jim was murdered, and Peter and Lady Jane are dead, they
were in Frost house when it burned."

"My God, how terrible," Molly asked.

"Yes, Meggie is here with me now, she had nowhere else to go. So,
she is staying with me for the time being."

"But the woman on the Altar Stone, what is happening?" Molly
said. "What is going on Brenda?"

"It was my Jim that was found on the Altar Stone. I have to go
now," Brenda replied. "I will talk to you later."

When Molly put down the phone, she told her husband the news.

"Peter and Lady Jane and Brenda's husband are dead," Molly
gasped and held on the to the side of the table. "All dead, I don't
understand what is happening here."

"Sit yourself down for a minute darling. I will make us some tea,"
Bert said.

"Thank you, Bert," Molly said. "I do feel a bit shaky."

They were devastated, but it was Alfie who had the greatest reaction. Molly was making breakfast when Alfie entered the kitchen.

"They are both dead, trapped in the fire," Bert repeated to himself. "I just can't imagine, what they..."

"Who is dead?" Alfie asked nervously.

"Peter and Lady Jane. Frost House burned to the ground yesterday," Bert replied. "With them inside."

"What a day, and now Father Jim murdered. Do they think it was arson?" Molly asked. "Meggie told me yesterday that Lady Jane was not well and had stayed in bed, but Peter?" Molly paused. "Poor Meggie."

"Peter is de... de... dead?" Alfie stuttered, he suddenly felt very confused, all these terrible memories were abruptly filtered back into his head.

"What is it?" Bert asked. "You look like you might faint."

Alfie could hardly speak and then he burst into tears. His head felt like it was going to explode, and he sat down and laid his head onto the table in front of him.

"Here, Alfie have a glass of water," Molly said. "Do you know something about this?"

At that moment Sofie entered the room in her dressing gown.

"Is it true? are Peter and Lady Jane dead?" she asked in quiet voice.

"I am afraid so," Bert said. "When the house burned down yesterday, and they were both inside."

"Oh my god," Sofie said. "How terrible."

"And Father Jim murdered," Bert said. "At the Altar Stone."

Sofie sat down heavily at the kitchen table and then she glared over at Alfie.

"You have to tell them about the thing they did on Friday," Sofie said. "Whatever it was. Peter was there, he was doing this ritual on the Altar Stone."

"What's this? Alfie are you involved in this?" Molly asked. "You must tell us what you know."

"I don't know. I can't remember anything clearly from Friday night," he said, raising his head from the table. "Peter blocks everything from our memory. But it is coming back. Oh my God Mum, I was there."

Molly looked at Sofie. "What is this all about?" she demanded.

Alfie started to cry again, and Sofie looked ashen as she glared at her brother. Alfie went even paler as the blood drained from his face; he was visibly shaking.

"You killed him. Did you kill Father Jim?" Sofie demanded.

"Okay, Sofie tell us what happened on Friday night," Bert said sternly. "Tell us now."

"Alfie invited me and Harry to go to the Altar Stone, he said that there was going to be a party. It was nearly midnight, but we still went, but there were only the four of us there, Peter, Alfie, Harry, and me. Harry was behaving very strangely, sort of out of it, if you know what I mean?" Sofie said. "I did not like it. Peter was talking about wealth and sacrifice or some such. I was really scared and then I fell over and Harry took me home." Sofie paused. "I really don't remember much more…"

"Peter uses mind control to get people to do things," Alfie suddenly said. "He is, I should say he was, very demanding, and if we did not agree to something, he would, somehow, make us do it anyway."

"So, that is why we can't remember things clearly," Sofie said. "What a dirty rotten bastard."

"Is this true Alfie? Did you lure Sofie and Harry to the Altar Stone. What were you going to do?" Molly asked. "And, how could you involve your own sister?"

"Alfie did you stay with Peter? Did you kill Father Jim?" Bert demanded.

"I don't remember clearly. But yes, I think Peter killed him. But we thought it was a woman."

"A woman?" Molly exclaimed. "But it was Father Jim?"

"Yes, but he was dressed up like a beautiful woman in a dress and everything. We did not know that it was Father Jim."

"My goodness. That explains a lot," Molly said. "I knew there was something not right in that household."

"I think we had better go to the police," Bert said sternly. "Get dressed now. Both of you."

Bert took Alfie and Sofie to the police station where they were interviewed by Detective Sergeant Brownload. It was then that the link was made with the death of Janice Spaiden five years previously.

After questioning, Sofie was allowed to go home but Alfie was held in custody, awaiting further investigations.

As the news spread around the village there was much speculation and gossip over the next few days.

"Can you believe it?" Gladys said as she was serving Tina in the grocery shop. "The murder and then Lady Jane and Peter dead in a fire. Meggie is distraught. She is staying with Brenda, so at least they can console each other. And I don't even know what to think about Father Jim dressed up as women! It's all so shocking. I heard that Alfie has gone to the police and is trying to tell them what happened. It seems that the poor boy is very confused," Gladys said. "They are holding him in custody."

"Yes, it makes me remember when my Janice died, they think there is a connection. She was very pally with those boys. The police came to see me yesterday and were asking lots of questions. They have also spoken to Harry to find out what he knew," Tina said, she seemed very upset. "I hate it that this is bringing back all those bad memories."

"At least the truth will out, and you will know what really happened," Gladys said. "How are you holding up?"

"I am okay." Tina shrugged. "When will it all end?"

"I am here if you want someone to talk to. It has to be better to get to the truth, Tina," Gladys said. "You must agree?"

 "That is true. But it is all so upsetting," Tina said. "Poor Meggie and Brenda. I would hate to believe that my Harry was involved."

"Hopefully the truth of it will all come out now," Glady's said. "It has been quite a week."

"It certainly has," Tina said as she left the shop. "Please don't let my Harry be involved in this."

Chapter fifty-three

When Jilly returned home with her sister Anne, after finding her sitting by the river, she phoned Alana.

"I could hardly recognize her, her hair was standing on end and her face white as chalk, eyes wild and unfocused. It was obvious that something had gone very wrong," Jilly said. "She is really worrying me."

Anne slept for over twenty-four hours before Jill could even try to talk to her.

"Anne," Jilly said, the following morning when bringing her sister, a cup of tea. "Do you remember anything about the day I found you by the river?" Jilly asked a few days later.

"I like the river," Anne mumbled. "We used to play making paper boats. Do you remember Jilly? We would put them in the water and then race down to the weir to see whose boat won the race."

"Yes, I remember, but that was over sixty years ago Anne. Do you remember last weekend?" Jilly tried over and over again, but Anne's mind was blank on anything after the war.

"My darling handsome Gerry will soon be back from the front, we have to get ready for my wedding, he will be here soon." Anne would put her hand to her hair, and then recoil from the touch. "What happened to my lovely hair?" she would ask, then she would look at Jilly in wonder. "Who are you?" she would ask.

"I am your sister, Jilly," Jilly would say.

"I don't know you," Anne would reply, but then she would go off into her own world again. Sometimes Anne became violent and would start screaming.

"The flames, the flames, they will devour me." Anne would tremble and cry out. "She made me do it. I didn't want to, but she made me."

Jilly was not sure before, but it became obvious that Anne had set the fire at Frost House.

"I think my sister is responsible for starting the fire at Frost House," Jilly said when she visited the police station.

"We will send out someone to question her," the desk sergeant said.

The following day a police officer arrived to talk to Anne, he could get no sense out of her, and suggested that a doctor be called.

When the doctor came to see Anne, he said a she was in a state of catatonia brought on by shock.

"She should go into a psychiatric hospital, she will be safe there," he said. "I will write up a report and let you have the names of suitable institutions."

After a few inspections and phone calls Jilly found a suitable psychiatric hospice and Anne was admitted the next week. Anne never regained her sanity, but she lived a relatively quiet life in the hospice until the day she died of a stroke some three years later.

Chapter fifty-four

A few weeks after the murder of Jim Noakes, Alana moved in with Jilly. Anne was in a psychiatric hospital, in Exeter, and Jilly did not want to move anywhere too far away from her sister.

"Are you going to continue running the shop?" Jilly asked Alana.

"I think I will. I have started to enjoy it. Business in Pandoras Box has really picked up, and I am getting a lot of mail order customers. I have decided to hire a manager to run the shop, so that I can concentrate on finding new merchandize and dealing with mail orders."

Alana had previously lived in the apartment above the shop and now that area could be turned over an officed and stock room.

"Why did you come here?" Jilly asked suddenly one Sunday morning, when they were sitting in the front room enjoying a mid-morning cup of tea. It was the room that used to be Anne's parlor, now re-decorated by Andy into a warm and cozy sitting room.

"You know why, when you contacted the Queen via the Moeston wiccan group, and asked for help," Alana said.

"No. I mean you once said that you had to atone for something and that was why you were sent here," Jilly said.

"Oh, it was something and nothing," Alana replied.

"Tell me about the something," Jilly asked.

"You really want to know?" Alana said.

"Yes. Because you know everything about me, my family and my family's history, but I know nothing about you."

"Okay," Alana said, "I once had a nice little house on the Summerset Levels, but it was compulsorily purchased for some new road network. I had to leave a lot of good friends and a reputable wiccan group behind."

"Could you not do anything to stop the road works?" Jilly asked.

"We tried, we obtained some rare spotted toads and put them in a pool on site. And then we tried to get the area designated as a Site of Special Scientific Interest. But it didn't work."

"Why was that?" Jilly asked.

"Well, they gathered up all the toads and moved them to another place. Quite near here, I believe. I think some have been seen locally."

"Yes, they have." Jilly laughed. "Where did you go then?"

"I went to stay in the Queen's house on Sloane Square, until I could decide where I wanted to live. Queen Emelia Rey's house is right next to Peter Jones, and I would often wander around the shops to pass the time. It was there that I first saw him," Alana said. "He worked in the household linen department."

"Him?" Jilly asked.

"Yes, he was a beautiful young man and I was smitten. I would go into the shop every day and I even started to follow him."

"Crickey Alana," Jilly said trying hard not to laugh.

"I know, it was a madness. Well, I did a glamour on him and I started to buy lots of towels and bed linen and the queen noticed.

It was hard not to notice with piles of towels and sheets turning up in the house every day."

"I bet," Jilly said with a grin.

"But you see the young man, Alistair his name was, he complained to his managers, and they obtained a restraining order, so that I could not go within three hundred yards of him. It was so embarrassing," Alana admitted. "It turned out that he was a homosexual, and I was really unsettling him."

"What happened?" Jilly asked, openly laughing now. "I am sorry," she spluttered, "but it is funny."

Alana grinned. "The Queen sorted it out and neither Alistair nor the store took any further action. But when your request came through asking for help, Emelia decided to send me. It was a good way of getting me away from an awkward situation."

"So, then you came here?" Jilly said. "I am glad that you did."

"And so am I." Alana said. "I adore you. you know that don't you?"

"I believe I do," Jilly said. "And I love you."

"And we will never be short of towels," Alana said with a grin.

Jilly and Alana lived together for twenty-six years, they were very happy and built up two good businesses between them, before they retired.

They formed a small but cosy wiccan group with the locals, that included Molly, Tina and Mr and Mrs Potts. Together they kept an eye on the goings on in the village.

Jilly died of a heart attack when she was eighty-three years old and Alana followed her two months later.

With the death of Anne and Jilly the Longland family line also came to an end.

Chapter fifty-five

Alfie was convicted on the charge of abetting a manslaughter and was given a ten-year sentence in prison. He had to received counselling to help him get rid of the bad dreams that plagued him after the murder of Jim Noakes and the death of Peter and Lady Jane.

Alfie admitted that Peter was involved in the death of Janice, he said, "that she died after Peter had had sex with her, she just stopped breathing, and we just left her on the stone." Apparently, Harry had been there earlier, but he had left before anything happened to Janice. "We had all had a lot to drink," Alfie said.

Harry was accused of abetting in the murder of Father Jim Noakes and Janice Spaiden, but Alfie contested that Harry had had nothing to do with the murders. So, Harry's case was thrown out of court, provided that he also had some counselling. Harry returned to university and when he graduated, he came back to the village and married Sofie Travas. They moved away to Bristol where Sofie opened her own dressmakers and repair business, it was called: Stitch and Sew.

The death of Lady Jane and Peter meant the end of the Frost blood line. Meggie collected the insurance money for Frost House and inherited what was left of the Frost fortune, and then she escaped to London to make a new life for herself.

One in which she could smile again, she knew that her Peter had tried to save Lady Jane, so he could not have been all bad. But she could no longer live in the village with the shadow of the murder hanging over her head.

"Its best if I leave," she told Brenda. "People will never forget. I think that I need to find a new place, somewhere I can make new and happy memories."

"I do think you are right. Make a new life for yourself," Brenda advised. "Try to put all this behind you. If you want to keep in touch, I will be here," Brenda said. "Do let me know how you are getting on Meggie."

"I will, and you take care of yourself," Meggie said. "Are you going to stay here? In the village, I mean?"

"Yes, I think I may. I have found something with Andy, that I had given up hope to find, and we are going to live together."

"That is wonderful, thank you for everything Brenda. Be happy."

"You too," Brenda said. "And don't be a stranger."

Chapter fifty-six

The following week Emelia Rey left promising to return. She left with two cars full of purchases. But before she left the village, she visited Jilly's workshop and selected a figure for her sculpture.

"I have not forgotten that I want that sculpture, can you have it ready for the Chelsea Flower Show in April next year?" she asked Jilly.

"Yes, that is no problem." Jilly said.

"Here is my deposit," Emelia Rey handed over five hundred pounds and an official order form. "Alana has asked me if she can stay here," Emelia said. "I would be very happy to see her settled here with you."

"Thank you very much, Emelia, I mean your majesty," Jilly said.

"Goodbye Jilly, I will see you soon. Just let me know when the sculpture is ready to be collected."

"I am sure you are looking forward to being home again," Jilly said.

"Yes, I am," Emelia said. "I miss my cat, Ebony, he will be pining for me. I hope they have kept him fed properly."

Hermana and Kigali heard this last comment.

"I hope he hasn't eaten anybody while we are away," Kigali quietly said to Hermosa.

"As do I." Hermosa said. "Let's get this shopping packed away and we can go home. I will be glad to be back in London."

Kigali was packing the last few things into the newly hired Bentley when Alana arrived. Emelia Rey had not been able to resist a few last-minute purchases and the car was full of luggage and bags of shopping. When he had finished, he went over to Alana and Jilly.

"We have enjoyed our visit to Little Barnstead. I am sure we will be passing this way again," Kigali said. "You two are meant for each other."

"Why thank you Kigali," Jilly said. "You have left behind a lot of admirers here. The village has never seen anything like it. You, the Queen and Hermosa, are the most glamorous people to ever hit the village."

Kigali laughed and went over to start up the Bentley, as he left, he waved to Jilly. Emelia Rey kissed Jilly on the cheek. "You are to look after each other," she whispered. "Goodbye Alana, keep in touch."

Hermosa approached Jilly and Alana as Emelia was getting herself ready to drive off in the Rolls Royce. Hermosa shook Alana and Jilly by the hand. "All the best to you both," she said. "Blessed be."

Alana put her arm around Jilly's shoulders. "We will do that. I promise you."

"We will," Jilly said. "Blessed be."

They stood and watched as the two cars disappeared down the road. "Perhaps we can have some peace around here now," Jilly said.

"I will drink to that," Alana agreed.

Chapter fifty-seven

Brenda had to vacate the church house when the new vicar arrived with his wife and took over the parish of Little Barnstead. Brenda and Andy lived in together in his little cottage.

"You will have to make me a larger kitchen," Brenda said.

"Your wish is my command, my darling," Andy answered.

Brenda soon found work as a teacher's assistant in the local school in Smalltown and Andy's business continued to grow.

"Do you want to say here?" Andy asked one morning.

"Surprisingly, I do, we can make a life here and you have your business. Is that okay with you?" Brenda asked. "We have made some good friends here and I feel settled."

"Yes, I just wanted to make sure that you were happy, that's all," Andy said. "I love you so very much."

"And I love you too," Brenda replied. "We can get away and travel as much as we like. Do you agree Terry?" she asked.

Terry barked twice in agreement and settled down in his bed in the swish new kitchen to gnaw on his bone.

"That settled then," Andy said.

In the summers they travelled all over the country with Terry beside them. There was some gossip when Brenda moved into Andy's tiny cottage. But it soon died down and the village became quiet as things gradually got back to normal.

As Brenda climbed on the back of Andy's motor bike, the motor bike that now had a snazzy new sidecar, perfect for Terry, who sat alert with his head poking out ready to the catch the breeze.

"Let's go and find somewhere a bit livelier for awhile, shall we? There is just is not enough going on around here," Brenda said.

The end.

About the Author

I have lived most of my life in North West London. I left school at 15 with no qualifications, and mildly dyslexic. I was a model in my teens and twenties, doing photographic and promotion work.

I went to Middlesex University in 1992 to study Spanish, Science and Technology for four years. I travelled extensively in Central and South America, including a nine month stay, studying at the University of Costa Rica. I spent a further six months travelling, eventually arriving in Trinidad and Tobago, where I wrote my Spanish thesis on the History of Carnival in Trinidad.

I was a qualified holistic therapist with my own practice in Hendon, providing massage and reflexology. I undertook a writing course with the Writers Bureau and have recently completed four short Open University courses, which I found very useful.

I write poetry and articles, having had several printed in magazines such as *The Lady*, *Prediction*, *Yours*, *Fate and Fortune*, *Here's Heath* and *Holistic Health and Healing*. I have also contributed to some anthologies and articles in some on-line magazines.

My first book: Can't Sleep Won't Sleep (Reasons and Remedies for Insomnia) took three years to research and write and was published in 2005.

My second book: Dreamtime (A History, Mythology, Physiology and Guide to the Interpretation of Dreams) was published in 2008.

My third project: Aphrodisiacs (Aphrodite's Secrets) on sexuality, sexual dysfunction, and the history and anecdotal use of aphrodisiacs from A-Z, was published in May 2009.

Aphrodisiacs and A-Z published by Skyhorse publishing New York.

Who Said that? (Meanings and origins of popular sayings)

Mystic Moon, (A history of the mythology, astrology and spiritual significance of the moon.)

I have also self-published four novels:

Rosie's Story (yes and pigs might fly)

African Nights (Georgina's story)

Earthscape (A long way from home)

The Arranged Wedding

The Story Tree (a collection of short stories and poetry)

Jokes (A selection of over a hundred jokes old and new)

(All available on amazon.uk)

African Nights (Georgina's story)

Georgina's life is in turmoil. A broken relationship, a passionate love affair, a life-threatening illness, her lover's disastrous trek into the wild lands of the Kalahari, and the trauma of realizing that she has made a great mistake – these are just some of the challenges she confronts in this gripping story. When Georgina's parents decide to take the family on a safari in South Africa, to celebrate their 40th wedding anniversary, they have little idea of the outcome.

Georgina meets Sammy, the enigmatic safari leader, and they fall in love. During Georgina's visits, she experiences the darker side of Africa when a boy is kidnapped and the culprits are found to be involved in obtaining body parts for witchcraft, and poaching rhino horns and ivory.

When Georgina finds that her skin cancer has returned, she does not go back to see Sammy as she had planned, telling him that it is over between them.

Sammy, devastated and losing all reason, drives off into the wild lands of the Kalahari Desert, where he runs out of food and water and is attacked by leopards. Dangerously injured, in shock and wandering in the desert, he is found by two San Bushmen who take him back to their camp.

Georgina hears that Sammy has disappeared and returns to Africa to help try and find him. It is then that she realizes she loves Sammy and cannot bear to lose him.

The book is based on a true story and gives a wonderful insight into the South African way of life, and an intriguing glimpse into the existence of the San Bushmen people of the Kalahari Desert.

Two reviews from amazon

"Exciting, passionate, compassionate, romantic, raw, gutsy, adventurous, exotic, real - this book takes the reader on a journey from cosy suburbia to the sunlit open spaces of Africa. The story works well on several different and equally effective levels, constantly surprising, sometimes thrilling, always heartwarming, nail-bitingly suspenseful and at times magical. Georgina's emotional journey is tumultuous, from a broken love affair to a new potentially devastating one with an outcome that seems to promise only more heartache, conflicting as it does with all she has ever known before. Yet the lovers - for this is essentially a love story writ large under hot skies - are so driven by their feelings that the impossible simply has to be made possible. I found this novel constantly entertaining, absorbing, at times intriguingly instructional and always totally engaging. Highly recommended!"

"I've just finished this wonderful book by Linda Louisa Dell, and must say I thoroughly enjoyed it. I found myself really involved in the character's life in South Africa where she faces a battle against skin cancer and there's a love story in here too. All very well written and compelling. Georgina's story is one of adventure and determination and I found myself fighting for her throughout the book. A great read."

Earthscape (A long way from home)

Stranded on Earth, two charismatic aliens, they seem to be benign, but are they, or do they have a more sinister agenda?

Kaximaki is devastatingly attractive, but young and naive; he gets left behind when his spaceship must leave suddenly to avoid detection by government agents.

He meets Katie a young Earth woman and they start their adventure together, as they flee the authorities and are hunted across Europe, with the help of Katie's friend Jayne.

His equally charming uncle is also stranded but is picked up by the authorities and held in a secure location.

Kaximaki's mother causes chaos back in his home world and the boys' presence on Earth, threatens to disrupt 'The Plan' that the aliens of the Tri-planet alliance have for Earth.

Their planet Tinka 17 is going to be sucked up into a black hole within the next few hundred years. They need a new home. Could it be Earth? But there are already too many people on Earth; a deadly virus could be answer, to reduce the population?

Two reviews from amazon readers:

"Linda Louisa Dells latest book is a revelation. It is well written and breeches that gap between 'normal' novels and science fiction. As a reader who did not do science fiction, I recommend this book to you as it has transformed my way of thinking. I could not put it down."

"'A look into the future and what could be. A kind of H.G. Wells. We can never be sure what awaits us in the years ahead - but it is comforting to know that there could be hope for mankind – beyond. All too often our view is to shoot and kill, then question afterwards."

The Arranged Wedding

"When third generation Asian girl, Leena, learns that her traditionalist parents have arranged a wedding for her with an Asian boy in whom she has little interest, a fascination sequence of events is set in motion which shows how very different such family arrangement are within the culture and context of modern-day England.

With a livery, sparky young female show has ideas of her own about her future. The twists and turns of the ingenious plot the well observed characters and the pace of the writing will keep the reader captivated and absorbed throughout, while the novel's resolution comes as a delight and a surprise. Strongly recommended."

(Robin Squires, author, and scriptwriter.)

"A charming, beautiful and funny modern-day story of love and cultural differences set against the more traditional background of arranged marriages.
A young girl, Leena Purri dreams of university and a career but this Is in direct contrast to her parent's wishes for her to marry a nice Indian boy of her parent's choosing. A series of events unfold Involving mix ups and misunderstandings leading both parents and Leena to re-evaluate what they really want in life to make themselves happy.
This well thought out and structured plot, characters and the style and pace of the narrative will keep you enthralled to the end. A highly recommended read!"

Rosie's story (Yes pigs might fly)

Rosie is a beautiful and sensitive woman; with three children by her violent and abusive husband. When the children grow up and leave home, Rosie also leaves; she just walks out one day and does not return, losing contact with her family. Living on the streets and witnessing many hardships and then running a homeless hostel. Her three children lead very different lives. Jill marries her childhood sweetheart, becomes a published author, continuing to live in the village where she was born. David goes to London and works in an engineering firm, meets his Jane, who has her own tragic family secret. Carla the youngest of the family runs off with a boyfriend to Greece and becomes part of a proud extended family that has some wonderful stories to relate. We follow the histories of these four, very different, characters their families and the people they meet along the way.

"A delightful, warm-hearted story that follows Rosie through life's trials, you can't help loving her and empathizing for her estranged family." (Patricia Santana, Mill Hill Book Club.)

"I found this novel impressive in so many ways, genuinely insightful as to the human condition, sometimes harrowing, always compassionate and ultimately uplifting." (Robb Squire, Ex-BBC script reader, published novelist and screenwriter)

"From the beginning you are immersed in the world of the Wilde family, from Rosie's harsh marriage and life on the streets, to the lives of her children as they make their way in the world not knowing the whereabouts of their mother. I particularly loved Carla's journey and the descriptions of her life in Greece. It's wonderfully emotive and in my opinion the perfect holiday read." (Lynne Chiles, writer, and lecturer.)

Rosie's, story, under the title of (Yes, and pigs might fly), was runner up for the best new fiction in the Wishing Shelf book awards 2012.

The Story Tree (a collection of short stories and poetry) by Linda Louisa Dell

Available on amazon at £9.99 book and £1.99 on kindle

Review and comments from readers of the Story Tree

"If you like your reading to be profound and written by a writer with a strong social conscience then you will love this eclectic volume." (Bookopedia)

"I was captivated. Every story is different, emotional, and sometimes very unexpected. A great read. Ideal for short journeys or long trips. You won't be able to put it down. Highly recommended. (Eliza Jane Goes. Published author)

I really enjoyed the varying lengths of the stories and poetry, and the completely random subject matters. The shorter, punchier tales were my favourites. I just kept reading until I had finished and then wished there were more tales to enjoy." (Robin Squire, ex BBC screen writer and author)

"Each branch of Linda Louisa Dell's Story Tree is a gem. Sometimes funny, sometimes unnerving, and often with an unexpected twist, this is a book that can be easily picked up and enjoyed whenever you want to relax with a good story. No matter what your taste, from the romantic to the downright scary, The Story Tree has something for everyone." (Amazon reader)

Linda Louisa Dell has also written four non-fiction books and four novels: Rosie's story, African Nights, Earthscape, The Arranged Wedding and a joke book.

For more information see her web page: www.lindalouisadell.com

Printed in Great Britain
by Amazon

83186871R00159